GROGAN'S STORY

40 YEARS A COP AND SOLDIER

MICHAEL GROGAN

CW03 MICHAEL GROGAN
(RET.) UNITED STATES ARMY

First Edition

PAGE PUBLISHING
Conneaut Lake, PA

First originally published by Page Publishing 2021

ISBN 978-1-6624-6004-3 (pbk)
ISBN 978-1-6624-6005-0 (digital)

Jan Ford, Editor
Cyndel Podich, Graphic Design

Printed in the United States of America

COVER PHOTO:
Grogan in a Chinook CH-47, Bagram Airfield, Afghanistan

For Officer Dave Chetcuti, Millbrae Police Dept.;

and Baby Sergio

Both taken far too soon.
Always in my heart.

CW03 Michael Grogan (RET.) United States Army

TABLE OF CONTENTS

HISTORY OF CHALLENGE COINS 10

CHAPTER 1 11
SAN JOSE POLICE DEPT. CADET
- ▶ Very dangerous, violent, and unpredictable
- ▶ My first murder victim
- ▶ A high-risk stop on a pickup truck
- ▶ All I wanted to do was to catch more
- ▶ Driving a police car in San Jose was living large
- ▶ My father and the Vehicle Code
- ▶ State trooper arrests terrorist bomber during traffic stop

CHAPTER 2 17
LOS GATOS POLICE DEPT.
- ▶ Arresting the straight-up drunk dentist in the rain
- ▶ Cruising and crime in downtown Los Gatos
- ▶ The famous tube top and the domestic violence arrest
- ▶ Rape, a yellow t-shirt, and burglary
- ▶ Police work from the rooftop
- ▶ Drunk is in jail after flicking lit cigarette
- ▶ The dome-light dummies snort cocaine
- ▶ Driving the car with the parking brake on
- ▶ Loaded guns, the Burger Pit, and landmark court cases

CHAPTER 3 25
MILLBRAE POLICE DEPT.
- ▶ Trying to fix the generation gap
- ▶ Pointing a gun at a baby
- ▶ Weird is normal and normal is weird on graveyards
- ▶ I knew I had to get out of the kill zone
- ▶ Hells Angels and the biker bar
- ▶ Pursuit of a carjacker
- ▶ The federal court system doesn't mess around
- ▶ The mystery of the uncooked hot dogs
- ▶ The one and only marathon
- ▶ Jenna Castillo the MMA fighter, Officer Rich Dixon, and me
- ▶ The WSIN helps arrest a Hells Angel
- ▶ My 15 minutes of fame and Avoid the 23
- ▶ Sergio the drowned baby and police grief
- ▶ A little baby boy was lying there, blue-gray and lifeless
- ▶ A severe state of emotional devastation and despair

- Suck it up, buttercup, is now out
- Grogan, stop shaking the car
- He fired several shotgun rounds into the fleeing car
- Cesar, the serendipitous K9
- A brain bleed, a missing tooth, and a severe black eye
- Why doesn't she just leave?
- The fight over medical records
- Domestic violence can happen anywhere, even on the freeway
- Patrolling my old beat for World Cup soccer
- The crazy high-speed pursuit
- We should have stopped the pursuit
- Go back? We were never there!
- 66 felony counts of child molestation
- Four pipe bombs and a large quantity of meth
- An egregious crime and an evil act
- Openly carrying machetes on their belts
- Dave's surreal on-duty murder
- Commanding the funeral honor guard
- What I learned from Dave's murder
- My mentor changed the CHP and helped establish POBOR
- Compromise and continuous improvement
- FBI National Academy and Compstat
- My mother self-medicated with meth

CHAPTER 4... 60
UNITED STATES COAST GUARD
- 12-hour police shifts propel me into the Coast Guard Reserve
- One of the Coast Guard's first sea marshals
- Climbing Jacob's ridiculously dangerous ladder
- Coast Guard screens crew, manifest, cargo

CHAPTER 5... 65
UNITED STATES ARMY
- Coast Guard blue to Army green
- B.U.M.-blame, understand, and minimize
- Deployed to Iraq, the wrong country
- The driver and the ground guide were best friends
- Iraq had become the proverbial hole
- A rocket landed about 20 yards from us
- The largest prison in the world
- Extremist organizations from Afghanistan, not Iraq
- *My official U.S. Army portrait.*
- Possibly trading jet fuel for alcohol in Afghanistan
- Joint Chiefs of Staff
- Protecting the top, top, top brass

- ▸ Visiting the amputee ward
- ▸ The story is that there is no story
- ▸ Celebrating when SEAL Team Six kills Osama bin Laden
- ▸ Promoted to Chief Warrant Officer 2
- ▸ Investigating widespread recruiting fraud
- ▸ Honoring Special Agent Sgt. Joseph Michael Peters
- ▸ The huge shoulder patch collection at the Globe and Laurel
- ▸ Delicious food and even better company

CHAPTER 6... 85
SAN MATEO COUNTY SHERIFF'S OFFICE
- ▸ Millbrae police disband and I become a deputy sheriff
- ▸ Rival gang members and 'the bucket'
- ▸ Catching a Caltrain vandal in San Francisco
- ▸ Meeting Medal of Honor Recipients
- ▸ More than a mile behind enemy lines
- ▸ Sneaking out of Bethesda Naval Hospital
- ▸ They collided head-on
- ▸ Removed from the car, placed on a backboard
- ▸ Extraditions to Ohio and Oklahoma
- ▸ Not a major tourist attraction
- ▸ Death by doctors
- ▸ When cops use any amount of force, it looks bad on TV news
- ▸ Asking the same question every day
- ▸ My sons, Jeffrey and Gregory, chose public service
- ▸ The police are the public and the public are the police
- ▸ His perfect combination of charisma and character

CHAPTER 7... 103
IN CONCLUSION
- ▸ Some semblance of peace and order
- ▸ Still pushing a patrol car
- ▸ Each use-of-force situation is unique.
- ▸ Police make most arrests without incident
- ▸ A smooth-talking, seasoned officer oozing with diplomacy
- ▸ Hard to get, easy to lose
- ▸ Adrenaline management
- ▸ Learning how criminals think
- ▸ Trying to fill the void

ABOUT THE AUTHOR................................... 110
ACKNOWLEDGEMENTS................................ 112

My grandfather, Arthur Grogan,
West Hartford, Conn. Police Dept.

GROGAN'S STORY

I was only 14 when I inevitably became fascinated with police work.

This surprised no one at all because I'm the son of a California Highway Patrol officer and a grandson of an officer with the West Hartford, Conn. police; both rode police motorcycles and so would I. The Grogan family's heritage continues: my brother was a police officer, my sister is an EMT, one of my sons is a fire captain in southern California, and the other is a local city police officer, also riding a police motorcycle.

Grogans just can't get away from public service.

My father, Richard Grogan,
California Highway Patrol,
San Jose Area Command.

History of Challenge Coins

According to the most common story, challenge coins originated during World War I. Before the entry of the United States into the war in 1917 American volunteers from all parts of the country filled the newly formed flying squadrons. Some were wealthy scions attending colleges such as Yale and Harvard who quit in mid-term to join the war.

According to another story, challenge coins date back to World War II and were first used by Office of Strategic Service personnel who were deployed in Nazi-held France.

Besides using coins for challenging, they are also used as rewards or awards for outstanding service or performance of duty. In that way, they build morale.

Today, challenge coins are popular among members of the U.S. military as well as with first responders. High-ranking military officers have challenge coins, as does the president of the United States. Recipients of the Medal of Honor also distribute their coins to important people.

Law enforcement and the fire service now use challenge coins to enhance agency pride, promote their respective departments and specialized units within a department. They are a lot of fun to collect.

There are many finishes available—from simple pewter to 24K gold. While there are only a few base metals, the patina can range from gold, silver, or nickel to brass, copper, or bronze plus the antiqued variations. Soft or hard enamel or a printed inset with an epoxy coating may add color. The epoxies are often more resilient and scratch-resistant than the metal surfaces.

Scattered through this book are a few coins from my collection. Each coin is treasured not only for its particular significance, but also for the memories and the honors they represent.

Chapter 1
San Jose Police Dept. Cadet

I signed up to be a cadet with the San Jose Police Dept. in California at 14 and started riding with police officers, then with the same graveyard shift with four officers and a sergeant, then with one officer.

I became a police cadet with the San Jose Police Dept. when I was only 14.

Very dangerous, violent, and unpredictable

From riding with the team, I moved to riding with the same officer, Hipolito "Hip" Delgado, a former Marine with great street instincts. Hip is my friend and mentor to this day. He was active in ridding the community of criminals, making his beat safe for perfect strangers to raise their families, work, worship, and go about their lives free of violence. At least that was the goal.

Even after decades of police work, I'm still impressed with the San Jose team's unwavering camaraderie. They had a balance of sarcasm and humor and were always playing practical jokes on each other. Come hell or high water, above all, no matter what, they always had each other's backs. I owe them for trusting me and putting up with me. I asked too many questions. I thoroughly enjoyed being even a small part of the team.

Police work was much more physical back then. Hands, feet, and batons were the personal weapons. There were no Tasers, bean bag rounds, pepper ball guns, pepper spray, or body cameras.

With only these weapons, as well as firearms, police work was even more challenging as phencyclidine, PCP, was very popular in San Jose and in other large cities. Parke Davis, now a subsidiary of Pfizer, designed PCP as an animal tranquilizer. On the street PCP was called KJ or rocket fuel. Sherms, named after a Los Angeles police officer whose last name was Sherman, were marijuana joints dipped in liquid PCP.

PCP suspects were very dangerous, violent, and unpredictable.

Police often responded to calls about guys running around without any clothes or jumping into swimming pools naked.

These weren't typical calls about indecent exposure, but someone reacting to being under the influence of PCP. The drug increases the user's body temperature, so they would try anything to cool down.

They were extremely difficult to deal with because they had a high tolerance for pain, or they didn't feel pain at all. It very often took many officers to subdue a suspect who was under the influence of PCP. Officers usually just dog piled on the suspect and hoped he tired out eventually. We often called this era the wild, wild West. I hope PCP doesn't make a comeback.

I was riding along weekly, even though cadets were limited to ride along once a month. I was also attending monthly meetings and working security details for high school football games at Police Athletic League Stadium and San Jose Earthquake soccer games at Spartan Stadium. The security details even paid $5 or $6 an hour.

The PAL Stadium was on the east side of San Jose where a lot, and I mean a crazy amount, of criminal activity was prevalent. Nearby was the notorious intersection of Story and King Roads, known as the East Side Knife and Gun Club.

Before the connector ramps were built, drivers on highways 101 and 680 had to drive through that dangerous intersection. Many didn't know they were traveling through a high-crime area fueled by rival gangs. Story and King was a popular place for gang members to cruise, play music, socialize, hang out, and kill each other.

My first murder victim

By the age of 16, I saw my first murder victim. The husband came home and interrupted his wife and her boyfriend. As the boyfriend was escaping over the back fence, the husband shot him in the back with a shotgun.

The boyfriend died in a gutter a block away. I will never forget watching the guy take his last breath. I helped with taping off the crime scene. Seeing someone take their last breath is one of the firsts we have in life that we never forget.

A high-risk stop on a pickup truck

One night there was a shots-fired call inside the Saddle Rack, a popular country western bar known for its mechanical bull like the one from the movie *Urban Cowboy*. As Hip and I drove up, we saw the suspect fleeing in a pickup truck and started to pursue him.

We made a high-risk stop when the suspect drove down a dead-end street. The suspect did not comply with Hip's verbal commands, so Hip took him to the ground and handcuffed him.

The suspect filed a complaint of excessive force and Internal Affairs investigators interviewed me. Ultimately, we were exonerated. Going to Internal Affairs was an intimidating experience and one I was able to avoid for most of my career.

All I wanted to do was to catch more

Another night, Hip and I responded to an alarm call at a liquor store. The front window was smashed and no one was around when we got there.

Hip said we are going to park down the street and wait for the thieves to return and get their loot. Sure enough, they did return, three of them.

We quietly drove up to them with the patrol car's lights out. Hip arrested two of them, and I was in my first foot pursuit after the third one. The suspect put up a pretty good struggle when I caught him. I ran cross country and wrestled in high school, so I was in good shape. I was so proud of myself. I single-handedly caught my first crook. All I wanted to do was to catch more. I could get used to this, I thought.

Hip taught me a technique that was never mentioned in the academy. Criminals really do return to the scene of the crime. This technique worked in a handful of other times throughout my career.

Driving a police car in San Jose was living large

Hip was patient with me and showed me the ropes. He taught me how to talk on the radio, eventually delegating most radio transmissions to me.

San Jose police allowed cadets to carry only handcuffs and a flashlight. I also carried a baton, Mace, and a radio. Once a lieutenant asked me why I was carrying a baton. I told him it was for protection and I never heard another word about it.

When I got my driver's license and things settled down, I even drove the police car. This was normally after 3 a.m. and only for a couple of hours. I was hooked. Driving a police car in San Jose was living large.

I was becoming immersed in law enforcement.

I gave tours of the San Jose Police Dept. on Sunday afternoons. These were typically groups of Girl Scouts, Boy Scouts, or members of local service clubs.

While a senior in high school I completed all four modules, A, B, C, and D, of the Reserve Police Academy through San Jose City College.

After attending high school during the day, I went to the reserve police academy at night from 6 to 10 p.m. Monday through Thursday. This went on for two consecutive semesters. I finished the entire reserve academy about the same time I graduated from high school. As a full-time student, I even made the Dean's List from San Jose City College, definitely not from high school.

My father and the Vehicle Code

My father, Richard Grogan, was a CHP officer assigned to the San Jose Area Command. I rode with him on Highway 17 in the Santa Cruz Mountains and saw how much he loved the variety and adventure of the job.

The CHP published a monthly magazine titled *The Highway Patrolman.* It showed graphic pictures of serious and fatal crashes. The magazine had a column called "Routine Stops," depicting not-so-routine traffic enforcement stops. All the drugs, weapons, stolen property, and other felony arrests from traffic stops were amazing.

I learned the value of using the California Vehicle Code as a tool to make stops. Down the road, I was frequently parlaying minor traffic violations into parole, probation, consent, and inventory searches leading into on-view arrests, just like my dad.

One of the most extreme examples of parlaying a minor traffic stop into a felony arrest happened in 1995, when Oklahoma State Trooper Charlie Hanger stopped Timothy McVeigh for missing a registration tag on his car.

State trooper arrests terrorist bomber during traffic stop

During the stop, Trooper Hanger noticed that McVeigh was carrying a gun and arrested him. McVeigh had just bombed the Oklahoma City, Oklahoma, Alfred P. Murrah Federal Building, killing 168, 19 of them children in the building's day care, and injuring 680.

McVeigh committed one of the deadliest acts of domestic terrorism in U.S. history. Only 90 minutes after the bombing, he was already in custody on an unrelated weapons violation stemming from a minor traffic stop. It became obvious that the Vehicle Code was the key to every criminal's heart and sometimes even the heart of a terrorist.

My father was a sterling example of what the CHP stood for. He performed his sworn duties with pride and unwavering dedication, finding it a privilege to make the highways safe.

He was riding his CHP motorcycle one morning in 1984 on a new section of the freeway with new asphalt.

He rode into a sinkhole through no fault of his own and was thrown off the motorcycle. Among other injuries, his right hand was broken. He had a heart attack during the operation to repair his broken finger. My father had to retire from a vocation he truly loved. I still remember looking forward to him coming home from the job and hearing his stories about his day

My paternal grandfather, Arthur Grogan, was a motorcycle officer in West Hartford, Connecticut, and, in 1944, died as a result of an on-duty motorcycle traffic collision when my father was only two.

Jason, my late younger brother, was a police officer in Capitola, California. His career was cut short, in part, after being injured in

foot pursuit of a parolee. He retired with a disability after 10 years on the job. My sister's oldest son, Kody, recently graduated from the San Jose Police Academy and is in the field training program. Her younger son, is a Navy SEAL attached to SEAL Team One.

My brother, Jason, a Capitola police officer, and me.

Chapter 2
Los Gatos Police Dept.

In October, 1980, one month after my 19th birthday, I was sworn in as a Los Gatos Police Dept. reserve officer. I went through a full field-training program, and in December I was appointed as a Level 1 reserve police officer, working alone and often getting paid.

The Los Gatos police patch depicts the two cat statues that guard a Los Gatos estate used as an artists' retreat. If you need to win a trivia contest one day, the names of the cats are Leo and Leona.

Arresting the straight-up drunk dentist in the rain

I had just passed the field training program and was working patrol alone when I made my first arrest for driving while under the influence of alcohol. It was raining as I drove north on Los Gatos Blvd. I saw a car in front of me speeding along at more than 50 mph in a 35-mph zone. I stopped the car at Los Gatos Blvd. and Lark Ave.

I walked up and asked the driver for his license. He handed me his racquetball membership card. I smelled alcohol. It became obvious the driver was not just under the influence, but straight-up drunk. He told me he was a dentist and close to home.

I asked him to step out of the car to take a series of field sobriety tests. He reluctantly agreed. Then he focused in on my youthful appearance, asked me if I knew what I was doing, and wanted to know how old I was. I didn't tell him my age, but assured him I was old enough to be a police officer. He did not like being detained by a kid.

The driver started making me nervous and made me doubt my opinion that he was actually drunk. I arrested him for DUI and drove him to downtown San Jose to the Alcohol Investigation Bureau, part of the county jail.

Fortunately, my CHP officer father just happened to be there with a drunk driver he arrested. Having my father there helped with my nervousness, knowing he would help me administer the Intoxilyzer test.

The dentist's blood-alcohol content was well over double the limit. Back then the limit was .10, unlike the .08 it is today. All in all, I stumbled to victory and acquired some confidence in my ability to spot and arrest drunk drivers.

Cruising and crime in downtown Los Gatos

On Friday and Saturday nights, downtown Los Gatos was a popular spot for cruising, bringing young adults and high activity from all over the South Bay. My partner and best friend Officer

Steve Mangin and I were assigned downtown in both uniform and plain clothes. Steve was hired when he was only 18.

Steve Mangin and me many years later as sheriff's deputies.

We complemented each other's style. Steve was calmer and a better report writer. I was on the hyper side and, happily, Steve liked writing most of the reports from the arrests we made. In other words, Steve was my anchor.

Steve and I did bar checks while neither of us was 21. Although we were covered legally, it seemed odd kicking minors out of drinking establishments when we too were minors.

The famous tube top and the domestic violence arrest

One afternoon I was dispatched to the Kings Court Shopping Center on a boyfriend-girlfriend dispute. When I arrived, they were still in a heated argument and the girlfriend slapped the boyfriend across the face.

I'd just seen a misdemeanor, so I handcuffed and arrested her. She suddenly took off running towards the very busy intersection of Blossom Hill Rd. and Los Gatos Blvd.

The big problem was she was wearing a tube top. A tube top has no shoulder straps, so as she was running, it slipped under her breasts, exposing her to the passing motorists. When I caught up to her I pulled her tube top up.

To say she was upset with me would be an understatement. I was even embarrassed for her. As it turned out, she was the granddaughter of a high-ranking Mafia boss. For the next month fellow officers who saw me would say "Move out of the way, dead man walking."

Rape, a yellow t-shirt, and burglary

On a Sunday afternoon, I was working patrol in a marked car when a report of a rape came out on the radio. The victim was washing her car in the driveway and went inside her house to take a shower. The suspect entered her house. He grabbed a knife from the kitchen.

He went upstairs and forced her out of the shower and onto her bed, where he raped her. She was able to provide only a vague description of the suspect: a Hispanic male wearing a yellow t-shirt.

As I approached the scene, I saw a shirtless Hispanic man walking down the street with a yellow cloth hanging out of his rear pants pocket. He denied any involvement with the rape, but I found a kitchen knife inside one of his socks when I searched him. The victim identified the suspect and the knife from her kitchen.

Police work from the rooftop

On another evening, Steve and I were working a plainclothes detail in an unmarked car. The Santa Clara County Sheriff's Office put out a be-on-the-lookout call for a suspect involved in a residential burglary. The only description was that the suspect was wearing waffle-stomper boots, which have an unusual sole design. The boots were very popular at the time. Obviously, the suspect left a footwear impression at the crime scene.

We soon saw a male subject walking towards us not too far from where the burglary occurred. I pulled the car over and grabbed the binoculars. Sure enough, he was wearing waffle-stomper boots. As he walked closer to us, he must have seen the binoculars and figured out we were cops. He suddenly sprinted toward a tract of townhouses.

I sprang into full foot-pursuit mode, but quickly lost sight of the subject. I decided to climb up on the roof of the townhouses and look down at the individual unit's patio. I saw a man on a patio. At first, I thought he lived there.

Then I realized that perhaps I made a poor decision by climbing on the roof. I identified myself as a police officer and began to tell the apparent resident who I was looking for. As I was politely talking with the subject, it dawned on me that he was the suspect with the waffle-stomper boots. He was apparently hiding in the patio to avoid me.

I pointed my gun at him and told him to lie on the ground. He did. I got off the roof and handcuffed him. Steve joined me and recovered stolen property that the suspect hid behind some bushes. We later learned the man had burglarized many homes. That was the first and last time I parlayed footwear impressions into a felony arrest. I wondered if the subject saw the irony in the situation.

Drunk is in jail after flicking lit cigarette

One particular evening we were conducting a routine bar check at Mountain Charley's. The bouncer told Steve there were some drunk guys in the bar, and he wanted them to leave. The drunks were stacking beer mugs 10 to 15 high.

We told the bouncer to tell the drunks they had to go or be arrested for trespassing. When the bouncer told the guys to get out, one of them flicked a lit cigarette at the bouncer's chest. That's assault and battery right in front of me, so I went to arrest the guy, and the fight was on.

Soon thereafter, two drunks were in custody and going to jail. There was some baton deployment, but neither one needed to be medically cleared before being booked into the county jail.

The dome-light dummies snort cocaine

We were regularly making on-view narcotics arrests on the weekends. Many of them were people parked in cars using cocaine. They were easy to spot because they turned on their dome light, unknowingly helping us to see what they were doing. We called them dome-light dummies. When we confronted them, the expressions on their faces were often priceless.

One Sunday afternoon, Steve and I were working foot patrol downtown. A Corvette was driving on North Santa Cruz Ave., its stereo so loud it could be heard from over a block away, violating a town ordinance. While the Corvette was stopped in heavy traffic, I walked up to the driver's door and saw he had an open can of beer between his legs.

I told him to pull over to the curb and he did, then I asked him to step out of the car and stand next to Steve while I searched the car for more open containers.

Behind the passenger seat was a little compartment. I opened it and saw a Ziploc baggie containing several paper bindles marked ½, ¾, and 1 gram. A white powdery substance resembling cocaine was inside the bindles with a combined weight of nearly 28 grams, or one ounce. That's a lot of cocaine.

Steve and I were worried that the search was bad because I was looking for more open containers, but found a good amount of cocaine instead. A regular officer joined us and assured us the search was valid. The white powder tested to be cocaine.

Because of the amount, the packaging and the markings on the bindles, we arrested the driver for possession for sale and transportation of cocaine. We booked him into the Santa Clara County Main Jail on the felony charges. The driver pleaded no contest during a preliminary hearing. A decent felony arrest, all from just a loud stereo.

Driving the car with the parking brake on

One evening we were in plain clothes and driving an unmarked police car. We pulled into the Foster Freeze parking lot on Main St. A guy walked up to Steve's side of the car and asked if we were interested in buying drugs. Steve said he was. The guy started to open the rear passenger door to get in the car. Steve told him to meet behind the car instead, concerned the guy might see the police radio mounted under the dashboard. The volume on the radio had already been turned all the way down.

As soon as the guy showed the drugs, Steve told him we were police officers and he was under arrest. The guy started to run. Steve grabbed his jacket. The guy slipped out of the jacket, leaving Steve holding it.

Well, I got a little excited and inadvertently jammed the parking brake release lever under the dashboard. As soon as I got out of the car I was in foot pursuit of the suspect. Steve got in the car and tried to release the parking brake but couldn't find the release lever.

Steve got on the radio requesting assistance, but no one was answering. In all the commotion, he forgot that the radio volume was turned all the way down.

He just decided to drive the car with the parking brake on and look for me. I was a block away and had just finished struggling with the suspect. I had him in handcuffs and was trying to catch my breath when Steve drove by. The engine was revved. Heavy smoke came from the rear tires. I tried to wave him down, but he didn't see me.

Ultimately Steve did find me. The suspect had a good amount of drugs. We booked him for selling controlled substances and resisting arrest.

Loaded guns, the Burger Pit, and landmark court cases

In September, 1981, Steve and I started the full-time police academy as reserve police officers. The Los Gatos police sponsored us. We wore the Los Gatos patch and received some ammunition for the range and the occasional use of a patrol car. San Jose police recruits made up most of the class.

Our class was the only one to use the old Samuel Ayer High School in Milpitas, Steve's alma mater. Even better, Steve's father owned the Burger Pit across the street from the high school turned police academy. You know where we had lunch every day.

One afternoon, Lucy Carlton, our tactical officer, called us into her office. She said she heard a rumor that we were going to the Burger Pit in uniform with unloaded guns, and that was unsafe. We quickly explained that our guns were actually loaded. We were already Level 1 reserve police officers, allowed to carry guns. We were the youngest in the class, and the only two recruits allowed to carry loaded firearms.

Police Academy graduation.

The Los Gatos police did not pay for us to attend the academy. Steve and I worked paid details downtown to have some income. We did foot patrol on Friday and Saturday nights. I worked the same detail on Sunday afternoon. We were extremely busy for six months. Steve also worked a lot of these details, but he had a part-time job delivering dairy products. We basically worked every day.

In class, we learned importance of landmark United States Supreme Court cases.

- ► *Mapp v. Ohio: Evidence obtained illegally may not be used against someone in a court of law under the Fourth Amendment of the Constitution, the amendment that covers search and seizure.*
- ► *Miranda v. Arizona: Law enforcement cannot use testimony given by anyone under interrogation while in custody without that person waiving their constitutional right to self-incrimination.*
- ► *Terry v. Ohio: It is not unconstitutional for police to stop and frisk a person they reasonably suspect to be armed and involved in a crime.*
- ► *Gideon v. Wainwright: States are required under the Sixth Amendment to provide an attorney to defendants who are unable to afford their own. That amendment insures a speedy and fair trial.*

Chapter 3
Millbrae Police Dept.

I became a full-time officer with the Millbrae Police Dept. in March, 1982, at the young age of 20. At about the same time, Steve joined the Palo Alto Police Dept. as a full-time officer. He was 21.

Millbrae is a small city on the San Francisco Peninsula. About 20,000 people live there. It's across the freeway from the San Francisco International Airport and bordered by the cities of Burlingame and San Bruno.

Millbrae was the only department I found that would hire police officers under 21. I worked there for 30 years, retiring at 50.

Trying to fix the generation gap

My first field training officer was Kenny Pacheco, a big Portuguese man and a strong former Marine. I was half his age, so there was an obvious generation gap. When I was driving the patrol car we didn't seem to have much to talk about. It became increasingly awkward. I came up with an idea to help break the ice. I picked up the microphone and said, "29 Paul 16 clear to 10-19," the code for return to the station, "and take a piss."

But the thing was, unbeknownst to Kenny, I unkeyed the microphone just before saying the "take a piss" part. Kenny immediately grabbed my right leg, just above the knee, and yelled, "You can't say that on the radio." Well, Kenny's grip on my leg hurt so much I started laughing uncontrollably. All I wanted to tell Kenny was I didn't say the "take a piss" part over the radio but I couldn't talk.

Eventually, after I regained my composure, I was able to explain to Kenny that I was only joking. He seemed to understand, I thought. This little stunt did actually work to break the ice and close the generation gap a bit. I didn't realize I would pay such a painful price.

A proud motorcycle officer with a lead wrist.

Pointing a gun at a baby

Armed robberies plagued the Peninsula in the fall of 1982. The robber was hitting businesses along El Camino Real, the main drag, or close to it. The only description was a white male wearing a blue bandana.

Millbrae police and San Bruno police shared the same radio channel at the time. During swing shift, San Bruno broadcasted that an armed robbery had just occurred at the Rib Shack, a restaurant on El Camino. The suspect was described only as a white male wearing that signature blue bandana. As usual, there was no vehicle description.

About a mile south of the Rib Shack, I parked my patrol car perpendicular to El Camino, on the south side of a Safeway store so that people driving south couldn't see me. I shined my high beams and spotlights towards the road to allow me to see the occupants of all the cars driving south. It wasn't too long before I saw a car driven by a white woman with a white man in the passenger seat wearing a blue bandana.

I pulled out onto El Camino and positioned my patrol car behind the suspect vehicle when I saw the passenger remove his bandana. It was too late. He was done.

After coordinating with other units, I made a high-risk or felony stop. All the other officers stayed behind their patrol cars with their guns drawn as I was giving verbal commands to the occupants.

The suspect got out of the car holding a baby in one hand and a handgun in the other. He pointed the gun at the baby and yelled for us to leave, or he was going to shoot the baby. I remember thinking "We never had this scenario in the academy, now what?" The stress factor had just doubled.

He stood near a large eucalyptus tree. A San Bruno officer got behind the tree and pointed his shotgun at the suspect's head from a distance of only a couple of feet. The officer told the suspect to drop the gun. He did. A woman officer ran up to the suspect and grabbed the baby.

The driver, the mother of the baby, was the wheel woman. We took her and the male suspect into custody without further incident. We turned the baby over to Child Protective Services. The suspect was charged with 11 counts of armed robbery and one count of kidnapping.

I was the investigating officer during the two-week jury trial.

During some of the court recesses the defendant, Gerald Edward King III, and I would have conversations. Somehow it came up that he was able to find out my Social Security number. I didn't believe him. I challenged him to prove it.

The next day, as I sat down next to the prosecutor, I saw a piece of paper with my correct Social Security number on it. I looked over at King and he just smirked. How he obtained my Social Security number I will never know. Of course, that was probably just the start of what criminals could find out about police officers' personal information.

Weird is normal and normal is weird on graveyards

I spent three years on the graveyard shift. Aside from the time I was on vacation, I was pretty much perpetually tired. At the time we worked eight-hour shifts from 11 p.m. to 7 a.m., five days a week.

Weird is normal and normal is weird when officers work graveyard.

Your circadian rhythm is totally out of whack. On the graveyard shift the calls for service were typically more serious and related to alcohol. There was hardly any traffic, so it was convenient to drive, or usually, speed, around town.

At least once a week, I would have an 8:30 a.m. court appearance that would continue until at least 11:30. If the case went to jury trial, that meant being awake all night and all day. Fortunately, I had a great sergeant who would let his officers sleep for two or three hours when things were quiet. Some sergeants would not allow sleeping on duty, period. I consider this short-sighted leadership. The San Mateo County Sheriff's Office, where I now work, provides sleeping quarters for employees who have extended commutes so that tired workers are off the road and safe.

On a good day, I would get four or five hours of sleep before going back to work. Sleep deprivation became a real problem. Functioning with less than six or seven hours of sleep is obviously dangerous. The chances of crashing the car or not being on your A game during a critical incident are very real. Lack of sleep definitely increases reaction time and clouds judgment.

People don't know how long an officer has been awake and how sleeplessness may contribute to an interaction. Law enforcement agencies must do more to address the problem of sleep-deprived officers. Sleep deprivation can play havoc with personal relation-ships as well. Some studies have shown that working nights is unhealthy and can cause long-term medical aliments.

I knew I had to get out of the kill zone

During the graveyard shift, county radio put out a broadcast of a white pickup truck traveling south on the 101 freeway from Brisbane, a few cities away up the Peninsula.

A man was shooting at vehicles with a rifle from the back of the truck. A San Bruno officer and I stopped a possible suspect vehicle on south 101 just south of Millbrae Ave. As we were commanding the occupants to show us their hands, the actual suspect pickup truck drove by.

The suspect shot out the left front tire of the San Bruno car. I pulled out behind the pickup just as it was coming to a stop near the Broadway Ave. exit. The suspect stood up in the bed of the truck and started shooting at me, hitting my windshield, bumper, and radiator.

I stopped and started backing up on the freeway. I knew I had to get out of the kill zone and I had to do it fast.

Several police cars from north San Mateo County were driving south on 101 and nearly crashed into me. The suspect continued shooting randomly at pretty much anything that was moving.

As one officer was stepping out of his patrol car, the suspect shot his light bar out. Another officer, who was standing against an apartment building wall, also came close to being shot when a bullet struck the wall only inches from him, raining broken stucco onto his head.

SWAT and negotiators responded and after several hours the suspect surrendered. As it turned out, the suspect vehicle ran out of gas and stopped at Broadway Ave. The suspect's girlfriend was driving the pickup. They were returning home from a meth-fueled camping trip. The suspect was paranoid and decided to shoot at all the cars "that were following him." This was the first and last time that I was shot at.

Hells Angels and the biker bar

While I was training a new officer, the two of us climbed onto the roof of a bar where bikers, including Hells Angels, used meth in the parking lot. The lot was full of motorcycles. We conducted surveillance from the roof. Hells Angels worked security at the front door. Bar patrons were drinking in an alley behind the bar.

We jumped a fence and walked around the block to get back to our patrol car so that we weren't seen by the patrons as they left. As we were walking by several apartment complexes, we heard multiple gunshots; we thought we were taking fire. At about the same time, we saw a car approaching us without any lights on.

The car made a right turn and sped up. I immediately broadcasted what we just heard and saw. Just by chance, there was a San Bruno patrol car driving on the same street and in same direction as the suspect vehicle. The San Bruno officer said he didn't see the suspect vehicle. I told him the car was directly in front of him. The officer turned on his emergency lights and began a long pursuit. The trainee and I made it back to our patrol car, and we began trailing the pursuit south on El Camino at 100 mph or more.

The suspect vehicle struck several other vehicles, but continued fleeing until it crashed into a light pole. We arrested the suspect and recovered a firearm.

It turned out that he had committed a drive-by shooting into a house over a gambling debt. However, he was one house off. He shot up the wrong house. If the trainee and I had not walked around the block to get back to our patrol car, we never would have spotted the suspect vehicle.

Dave and me with our Millbrae patrol car.

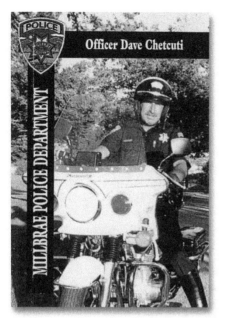

Officer Dave Chetcuti

Officer Chetcuti began his career in 1983 with the Millbrae Police Department as a Reserve Officer. He became a full-time police officer in 1987. Since that time, he has been a Field Training Officer, Acting Watch Commander, Equipment Officer, and is currently assigned to the position of Traffic Officer. Officer Chetcuti's interests are fishing, boating, and classic cars.

Sponsor:

SERVICE MASTERS
Millbrae
583-5513

You can help keep roadways safe by being a good defensive and responsible driver.

© 1998 House of Steno, Inc • 1-800-479-6062

Millbrae police carried trading cards. This is Dave's.

Pursuit of a carjacker

On September 1, 1993, Officer Dave Chetcuti, who would be murdered on duty in just a few years, and I were working the day shift. County radio advised of an armed carjacking that just occurred in Fremont, a city on the east side of the San Francisco Bay. The suspects were driving west over the San Mateo-Hayward Bridge towards Millbrae and crashed near Magnolia Ave. and Trousdale Dr.

They were last seen running north towards Murchison Dr. and El Camino. Dave and I began an area search. There were telephone repairmen up in a cherry picker in front of a nearby Lyons restaurant. One of the linemen saw us, pointed at Lyons and shouted "They just ran into the restaurant."

Dave and I went in and saw the two suspects sitting in a booth, obviously out of breath. An employee said one of them ran into the restroom before sitting in the booth. Dave went into the restroom and found jewelry stolen during the carjacking in the bottom of the trash can. The suspects were charged under the recently enacted federal carjacking statute.

The federal court system doesn't mess around

Officer Max Bosel and I separately stopped a suspect in 1994 for traffic violations and arrested him for possessing a loaded and concealed firearm. We learned that the federal Drug Enforcement Agency had the suspect under investigation under Operation Target for distributing large amounts of tar heroin.

The suspect was a member of a Mexican drug cartel and had a safe house in Millbrae. A safe house is a secure location suitable for hiding drugs, weapons, and other contraband. The suspect and his associates primarily operated in the Mission District of San Francisco.

Max and I testified in the suspect's jury trial in the U.S. District Court, Northern District of California the next year. There was a suppression hearing to determine if we had probable cause to make our respective traffic enforcement stops.

Max testified that he was working radar and stopped the car for speeding. I testified that I stopped the car for being too low to the ground and having tires that were too small, creating an unsafe vehicle. Because the driver was wearing gang clothing and had visible gang tattoos, for my own safety I asked him to step out of the car where I pat searched him. I found a loaded and concealed firearm in his waistband.

The judge ruled that the traffic stops were based on probable cause. The firearms that were discovered from legal stops were admitted into evidence.

The jury convicted him on multiple counts of controlled-substance violations, including a heroin conspiracy charge and a charge of continuing criminal enterprise. He was sentenced to 290 months in prison on the conspiracy charge and 420 months on the continuing criminal enterprise. The court ordered the sentences to run at the same time. The continuing criminal enterprise got him an extra 10 years in prison for each firearm arrest Max and I made.

The federal court system doesn't mess round.

The mystery of the uncooked hot dogs

A neighbor called the police reporting a suspicious male looking over a gate and into a backyard. The dispatcher described the subject, and a couple of officers and I located a man who matched the description.

He was walking a few blocks away from the scene, carrying a brown lunch bag. When we confronted him, he told us his name, but said he didn't have any identification. We patted him down and found he was carrying a concealed loaded semiautomatic firearm. We handcuffed him.

I looked into the brown bag and saw two packages of uncooked hot dogs. The suspect explained that he had the hot dogs so he could give them to the students for lunch at the nearby Mills High School. This made absolutely no sense.

After a lot of conversation, the subject revealed he was actually a police officer assigned to a narcotics unit. He gave consent for us to go into his truck, which was parked nearby, and get his police identification.

We confirmed he was a police officer, and he admitted to initially giving us a false name. It turned out that he and other members of his unit recently executed a search warrant at the house where he was seen looking into the backyard. The hot dogs were supposed to distract the dogs in the house while he retrieved money he had hidden in the house during the execution of the search warrant.

We reported him to the district attorney's office for giving false information to a police officer. A supervisor from his agency came to the Millbrae police station and took the officer into custody. He was assigned to the records bureau while an Internal Affairs investigation was conducted.

The one and only marathon

In 1994, Steve and I decided to run a marathon together. We chose the Avenue of the Giants Marathon in Humboldt County in northern California. The county is a beautiful place with a great many towering redwood trees. It is one of the most scenic marathons in the world. The Humboldt Redwoods Marathon is run on the same course but in the opposite direction.

Steve and I began our training regimen about six months before the marathon. Steve was living in Bend, Oregon, and I was in Millbrae. A lot goes into training for a marathon. We talked almost every day as we trained. We worked ourselves up to monthly long runs of 18 or 20 miles, and incorporated speed work on 400-meter tracks.

Learning how to pace oneself correctly for race day may be the absolute most important element for success.

I did not pace myself.

Steve and I were always competitive. My desire to beat him overtook my training and I paid the price for it. I started off way too fast and by the 13-mile marker I was in so much pain I started to cry. I went too fast and died a slow death.

Before the race, I knew it was important to hold back during the first part and run smart. Steve and I did finish the marathon. I didn't finish strong, but I did finish. I ended up with a stress fracture in my foot that lasted for months. Nevertheless, it was a great personal accomplishment for both of us. This was our first and last marathon.

Jenna Castillo the MMA fighter, Officer Rich Dixon, and me

In March, 2019, there was an International Women's Day conference at the Maple Street Correctional Center in Redwood City. Jenna Castillo, a mixed martial arts fighter, was the guest speaker.

Jenna told the attendees that two Millbrae police officers, Rich Dixon and I, were instrumental in helping her and her mother. She said her biological father was a heroin user and dealer who went to prison. Jenna was young and hasn't seen her father since.

Jenna's mother was also a heroin user and worked at the Safeway grocery store in Millbrae. Rich and I worked part time there as store detectives and became friends with Jenna's mother. We persuaded her to move to Millbrae so Rich and I would be able to help her and her daughter stay away from negative influences.

It wasn't until several attendees at the conference told me about Jenna's story that I realized the impact we had on her and her mother. Jenna and I reconnected and she shared her story with me. Jenna's mother was able to stop using heroin and focus on raising Jenna. I never realized or imagined that this relationship with Jenna's mother would result in such a positive and long-term change for Jenna and her mother.

Jenna never used drugs and started studying karate at the age of eight. Later she became an MMA fighter and competed around the world. She even competed at the Playboy Mansion in Beverly Hills. Hugh Hefner was there watching. Jenna now has a two-year-old daughter and teaches martial arts. Jenna and her mother are best friends.

The WSIN helps arrest a Hells Angel

One afternoon, I walked out of the Millbrae police station to go to lunch downtown when I saw a Hells Angel riding a motorcycle, wearing a leather jacket with three patches on the back. There was a top rocker with the words Hells Angels, a bottom rocker with the words San Francisco and in the middle was the famous and copy-righted death's head.

The motorcycle was excessively loud. I motioned for the Hells Angel to pull over and stop and immediately called for patrol officers to meet me. I issued him a citation for excessive noise.

When I got back to the police station, I phoned the Western States Intelligence Network and requested a check on the Hells Angel. WSIN is a law enforcement information-sharing system that helps officers identify suspects in mutual investigations. There was a hit on the Hells Angels' name. I was directed to phone a specific detective with the Las Vegas Metropolitan Police Dept. for more information. The detective told me that Las Vegas police had recently arrested the Hells Angel for selling cocaine. This information was interesting, but not particularly helpful.

During the conversation, the detective mentioned he was trying to identify a guy with full arm, or sleeve, tattoos using the name of a deceased person from Redwood City, about 12 miles from Millbrae.

Out of a one-in-a-million chance, I thought of a former Hells Angel who grew up in Millbrae. I was very familiar with him; I knew he had sleeve tattoos and had moved to Las Vegas. I also knew he had a $500,000 arrest warrant out of San Francisco Police Dept. for driving his truck into his girlfriend's bedroom. The girlfriend was not injured. I sent the detective a picture of the guy. Sure enough, it was him. The next day the detective arrested the guy for the active warrant.

My 15 minutes of fame and Avoid the 23

I became quite the media star on television news broadcasts during the several annual three-week Avoid the 23 Christmas and New Year's police crackdowns on drivers who were under the influence of alcohol or drugs, or in some insanely dangerous cases, both.

Avoid the 23 was a grant program funded by the California Office of Traffic Safety through the National Highway Traffic Safety Administration. It was named after the 23 law enforcement agencies in San Mateo County and aimed to reduce the numbers of injuries and deaths caused by impaired drivers.

The Bay Area Avoid Campaigns shoulder patch graphic designed by Cyndel Podich, the graphic designer of this book.

The grant funded officer overtime, police DUI strike teams, sobriety checkpoints, and a highly successful public information component that achieved saturation coverage in the extremely sophisticated San Francisco media market and won 35 law enforcement and public relations awards.

On camera with television news crews.

Our public information director, Jan Ford, put me on television, on news radio and in newspapers regularly. My TV news segments drove Jan crazy. I tend to sway from side to side on camera. She told me repeatedly to stand still, but it's not in my nature.

I had cut my face shaving just before one TV interview, and the wound would not stop bleeding. Can't go on TV like that, so Jan marched me over to the drug store just across the street from the police station and I bought a styptic pencil to stop the bleeding. It stopped it, all right, but stung like mad. The things we do for fame.

In fact, San Mateo County pioneered the concept of regional multi-jurisdictional DUI strike teams operating on the holiday weekends, when DUI arrest numbers soar.

Our teams consisted of 20 to 30 officers from jurisdictions in the southern, central, or northern sections of the county. Millbrae joined the highly competitive central team.

After our team briefing and pizza dinner and wearing our Avoid the 23 raid jackets, we took to the roads and freeways on the hunt for DUI suspects. I was in a patrol car on 101, my eyes on a swerving car ahead of me that had a broken tail light. Just as I was about to pull the car over, a CHP unit swooped in front of my car and made the stop. Competitive indeed.

I tried another stop, this one without the CHP. As Jan and I drove down an onramp to 101, I saw a car parked with its doors open and two people in the roadway on the passenger side of the car. The man was beating up on a woman. I arrested him for domestic violence and DUI. Not just a drunk driver, a violent one.

Other counties in the San Francisco Bay Area now use the concept and, in our county, we kept the regional strike teams and focus them on other crimes.

Sergio the drowned baby and police grief

I have seen the psychological effects of death and dying among family members of the dead throughout my career, and have found myself personally and emotionally caught up in the investigations.

I view every day as a gift and have learned not to take life for granted. I have tempted fate many times and wonder how I lived to tell the tale. I have seen more than my fair share of death, which is probably typical for a career in law enforcement. I have investigated murders, fatal traffic crashes, suicides, and death from natural causes.

I have attended many police funerals and many ceremonies across the street from the State Capitol in Sacramento when the names of fallen officers from the previous year are enshrined on the California Peace Officers Memorial. I also attended similar ceremonies at the National Peace Officers Memorial at Judiciary Square in Washington D.C.

Many police officers can't stand hearing the hymn "Amazing Grace," because it is almost always played at police funerals, most often on bagpipes. The pipes are used to honor the historical British Isles origins of many early police officers.

To this day, one particular death investigation haunts me. I became emotionally involved with this tragedy and still haven't found closure.

A little baby boy was lying there, blue-gray and lifeless

It was a quiet Saturday afternoon when I received a radio call of a one-year-old baby who drowned in a hot tub. This was the first, and to this day the last, time I ever started shaking from being dispatched to a call. I arrived at the house within minutes and was immediately confronted in the kitchen by several agitated, emotional adults.

I saw a little baby boy lying on the floor, looking blue-gray and lifeless. For a split second I thought the baby could even be dead. As the firefighters arrived on scene, I knew it was our duty to save the baby.

As I reflect back on the situation, I knew the baby was dead. Maybe if the hot tub were filled with cold water the baby would have had a chance, but the water was over 100 degrees.

I touched the baby to locate a pulse, but didn't feel one. He felt unusually hot. I immediately began cardiopulmonary resuscitation. The firefighters assisted me soon after.

We decided to drive the baby in the patrol car, with emergency lights and sirens, to the nearby Peninsula Hospital's emergency room. I drove the police car to the very best of my ability while getting the baby and firefighter safely to the hospital. The firefighter continued to perform CPR.

The baby regurgitated during the ride, a strong odor I occasionally smell in my head to this day. It's like the distinctive stench of the morgue. Smell it once; it's with you forever. I took this involuntary bodily function as a good sign and really started to believe that the baby wasn't going to be cheated out of life.

Once we arrived at the hospital, several doctors worked feverishly on the baby. After 45 minutes, the doctors pronounced the baby dead. The doctors met the parents in the waiting room and apologized for not being able to revive their son. The father started screaming and asked if he could see his son. The doctors escorted him to the resuscitation room.

A severe state of emotional devastation and despair

I saw the father pick up his son from the gurney and hug him as if he were just born. He then began to cry uncontrollably and yelled, "No Sergio, no Sergio, you can't leave me," while running around in the ER.

At this moment, for the first time since I became a police officer, I too began crying with the father. My sympathy for the family was total, and I was no longer able to deny my very first impression that the baby was dead. If I were the father, I would also be in a severe state of emotional devastation and despair.

I returned to Sergio's house and began a death investigation. A relative of baby Sergio drove up to the house the same time I did. He asked me if the baby was okay and I began to cry again. I believed the answer was obvious. He told me Sergio was not dead. He was only a baby; he could not die. I wished with all my heart this was the case.

My investigation revealed that baby Sergio's father, Sergio Senior, and the baby were in the back yard. The father fell asleep on a lounge chair and when he woke up he looked around the back yard for the baby but couldn't find him.

He finally found his son at the bottom of the hot tub. He pulled him out. The baby was unconscious. The father called 911. Afterwards, I went to the station and cleaned the inside of the patrol car.

I never attended Baby Sergio's funeral, but wish I had.

Suck it up, buttercup, is now out

Back then, first responders were not given the opportunity to go through the grieving process. Stress accumulates; it is fortunate that things have changed. We now have peer counseling, formal counseling through employee assistance programs, and other counseling that first responders feel comfortable using.

First responders are no longer looked down upon for seeking help after being confronted with traumatic situations. The outdated adage of "Suck it up, buttercup" is now fortunately universally recognized as counter-productive.

There was an investigation into our decision to drive baby Sergio to the hospital in the police car rather than waiting for the ambulance to arrive at the house. It turned out we arrived at the hospital about the same time the ambulance would have arrived at Sergio's house. We made the right call.

After I wrote the report, I went back in service.

I remember not being able to focus and being emotionally preoccupied for several months. By the grace of God, I was able work though this tragedy alone. I never thought about reaching out for the help that, looking back, I clearly needed.

Critical-incident stress debriefings are becoming normal. They bring together most if not all those who participated in a serious incident that typically involves death, major injuries, children, active shooters, or other horrific situations first responders are called upon to resolve.

For a long time, police dispatchers were left out of these debriefings, but that has changed. Dispatchers are the vital link between the public and first responders. First responders could not perform their duties without them. It is difficult to find closure for the serious calls for service that dispatchers handle. More often than not, dispatchers don't know how calls end.

Stress debriefings allow dispatchers to explain how they felt during a critical incident and to learn the resolution. As Lt. Col. David Grossman would say in his book; *On Killing*; "Pain shared is pain divided" and "Joy shared is joy multiplied."

Grogan, stop shaking the car

On October 17, 1989, the San Francisco Giants and Oakland A's were playing game four of the World Series in San Francisco's Candlestick Park.

I was working swing shift and training a new officer. We were in downtown Millbrae when the Loma Prieta earthquake rocked much of Northern California. The World Series was delayed for several weeks. When the series resumed, the A's ended up sweeping the Giants.

I was standing outside and talking to a senior officer who was sitting in his patrol car. My hand was on the roof of the patrol car when it started rocking from side to side. The officer said, "Grogan, stop shaking the car." We both then saw Broadway rolling and buildings violently shaking.

There was no doubt this was a major earthquake.

My infant first son, Jeffrey, and my wife, Donna, were at her parents' house in Millbrae. I told my trainee to drive lights and sirens to their house to check on them. I ran into the house and found Jeffrey asleep in his crib like nothing ever happened. He slept right through the magnitude 6.9 earthquake. What a relief and an overreaction of a new father.

Among other reports of major damage and fires, we learned that that a major portion of the double-decker section of the Nimitz Freeway in Oakland known as the Cypress Structure collapsed, killing 42 people.

He fired several shotgun rounds into the fleeing car

Early one morning, I was leaving the county jail in Redwood City when dispatch advised of an alarm at a 7-Eleven. We seldom hear alarms from this particular business, so when we do, we consider them valid. I stepped up my response back to Millbrae when the first officer on scene said that a robbery had just occurred.

The suspect was armed with a knife and had a T-shirt pulled over his head. He was last seen running towards the alley behind the 7-Eleven.

A car drove right at the pursuing officer as he got to the alley. The officer jumped out of the path of the car and fired another round at the back of the car, striking the trunk lid. The first two rounds went into the windshield, went up and came to rest in the headliner of the roof. The third round went through the trunk and the back seat and came to rest on the driver's seat, only inches from the driver.

As the sergeant arrived on the scene, he fired several shotgun rounds into the fleeing car. A long pursuit ended in South San Francisco where police arrested the suspect.

Right after sunrise, I was taking pictures and drawing a diagram of the side of an apartment building that was hit with some shotgun pellets. A lady on the second floor opened her window and asked me if anything was wrong. I told her everything was okay. She had to be a very sound sleeper.

In July, 1991, Millbrae police were called upon to investigate two murders that happened on the same day. Both victims were 22-year-old white men, both shot to death, their bodies found fairly close to each another. Was this a bizarre coincidence or the work of the same gunman? After years of investigation, we determined the murders were unrelated, but neither murder has yet been solved.

Cesar, the serendipitous K9

Another detective and I responded to an interrupted residential burglary while we were assigned to the investigation bureau. We helped establish the perimeter, taking up a position in a park that was down a hill and a couple of blocks from the burglarized home.

A woman pushing a baby stroller with a German shepherd dog on a leash happened to walk by. We identified ourselves and told her why we were in the park. Kind of jokingly we asked if her dog were able to help us catch some bad guys. To our surprise, she said, "Yes, he's a police dog." She went on to tell us she was Officer Anne Dickson, a K9 handler from a nearby police agency, and this was her work partner, Cesar.

She told us she would be willing to help us out, but she needed someone to watch her son, who was in the stroller. About that exact time, my wife, Donna, happened to be driving by. I waved for her to stop and she did. I asked her if she could babysit for a little bit and she agreed. I asked Officer Dickson if she would be comfortable with my wife watching her son while she and Cesar went to work. She said she would.

The handler and the dog started to walk up the hill, which was covered with thick vegetation and tall trees. Cesar started barking and searching. It wasn't too long before we heard over the radio that the suspects were running away.

The timing of the K9 handler and her partner walking by the park, along with my wife randomly driving by just moments later was serendipitous. We believe the suspects gave up their position inside the perimeter and ran when they heard the dog barking. Two burglars went to jail.

A brain bleed, a missing tooth, and a severe black eye

When I was a detective sergeant, I read a police report of domestic violence. The female victim was admitted to Peninsula Hospital, where she was treated for a brain bleed, a severe black eye, and a serious bruise on her right arm.

Hospital staff are required by law to report this crime, so when the victim was being admitted, staff notified Millbrae police of a suspected act of domestic violence.

A Millbrae officer met with the victim at the hospital. She told him she was hurt when she fell while walking to the dentist's office. The officer then phoned the victim's husband and inquired about his wife's injury. He told the officer he thought his wife fell while walking on El Camino, but wasn't positive how she got hurt. The officer wrote in his report that he couldn't tell who was telling the truth.

From the limited information I had at the time of reviewing the report, I thought neither the victim nor the husband told the truth. I took it upon myself to find out.

In the mid-1980s, California, like many other states, made domestic violence cases of the utmost importance, turning them from misdemeanors into felonies. This allowed officers to make felony arrests for domestic violence assaults that did not occur in their presence.

Just for the record, officers may make arrests when a misdemeanor happens right in front of them. Felonies do not need the police presence.

The statute changed the way law enforcement dealt with this violent crime. It had previously been mostly ignored, or even actually condoned. The new law also made it mandatory for officers to make arrests in domestic violence or spousal abuse cases.

Probably the most important reason for the passage of such a strong law was to break the cycle of violence.

When I started police work, domestic violence cases were often handled with no paperwork. Typically, the woman and the children were driven to her parents' house for the night. The husband, usually the primary aggressor, was driven to a hotel or friend's house for the night. The strategy was merely to separate them.

Case closed.

Once the enhanced laws went into effect, police officers were tasked with helping to break the cycle by making the arrest required by law.

Why doesn't she just leave?

At first, people, including police officers, would ask, "Why doesn't the victim just leave?" The reality is that the dynamics are extremely complicated. Victims, particularly women, can easily become caught up in a cycle that makes it nearly impossible for them to break away from a dangerous relationship.

We provide victims with information that allows them to talk with counselors about financial assistance and alternative housing options, among other available resources. This process also forces the batterer to look at his criminal behavior.

The court now orders that the batterer seek domestic violence counseling. Batterers are now issued domestic violence emergency protective orders against them when they are arrested. This allows for a cooling-off period between the victim and the batterer. Police take the batterer's firearms for safekeeping until a court order releases them.

During my investigation, I interviewed the husband several times. He finally told me that he caused the bruise on his wife's arm. He said that one night he heard his wife fall down the stairs and he immediately checked on her. He picked her up off the floor by grabbing her right arm and helped her back up the stairs and into bed. The next morning, he saw that his wife had a black eye, a missing front tooth, and a bruise on her right arm where he grabbed her. The husband then drove his wife to the Peninsula Hospital emergency room.

I told the wife about her husband's most recent account of her injuries. She also changed her story and said she did fall down the stairs.

I consulted a physician who worked at the county hospital, showed him Polaroid pictures of the victim's injuries, and asked him if the injuries fit with falling down a flight of stairs. The doctor said that the black eye was most likely caused by being punched or being hit with a baseball. He said that if the victim did fall down a flight of stairs, there would be abrasions on her face and even on her arms.

The fight over medical records

I asked the victim if she would sign a release form allowing me to obtain her medical records. She reluctantly signed the form. However, once the husband found out his wife signed the release form, he went to the hospital and had her rescind it.

Now, my only recourse in getting the medical records was to get a search warrant. After I got one, I made a courtesy call to the hospital records department to let them know I would be there in a couple of hours to get the medical records. The records manager told me she would not be able to release the records until the hospital's legal department reviewed the search warrant.

In the nicest way possible, I tried to explain to the records manager that she really can't deny giving the medical records to me now that I have a search warrant. She still didn't understand. I told her that if the medical records were locked in a safe, and they didn't give me the combination, I could use a blow torch to open the safe.

Well, this hypothetical example didn't work.

She called the chief of police and reported that I threatened to blow up the hospital. Ultimately, and after a fair amount of persistence, the records manager provided me with a copy of all the medical records.

I was able to get an arrest warrant for the husband for spousal abuse. The judge set the bail at $100,000. I went to the couple's apartment, arrested the husband and booked him into the county jail.

When it came time for the trial, there weren't enough courtrooms available and charges were dropped. Even though I was frustrated, I knew I did everything I could do for the victim. Prosecutors proceed with criminal charges even if the victim is unwilling to cooperate.

Domestic violence can happen anywhere, even on the freeway

Early one dark morning I was driving back to Millbrae from the county jail on 280. As I approached Trousdale Dr. I saw a car parked in the center freeway divider with no lights on.

I stopped behind the car. It looked empty. I walked up to the driver's door to stay as far from the traffic lane as possible and saw a man punching a woman who was balled up on the right front floorboard. He punched her several times in the head and face.

I opened the driver's door, pulled the man out of the car, and handcuffed him. A few minutes later a CHP patrol car stopped to help. The CHP officers drove her to nearby Peninsula Hospital and I drove him to the county jail where he was booked for assault and battery. The investigation revealed that this incident was the accumulation of a boyfriend-girlfriend dispute that turned violent.

Patrolling my old beat for World Cup soccer

When the U.S. hosted the men's World Cup soccer tournament in 1994, Stanford University was one of the country's nine venues. The town of Los Gatos, 17 miles away, became the unofficial headquarters for the Brazilian World Cup soccer team and fans. I had been a police officer there 12 years ago.

Celebrating each victory, Brazilian visitors and residents would congregate downtown, drawing crowds in the thousands.

In anticipation of the Brazilian soccer team advancing in the tournament and Independence Day approaching, the Los Gatos Police Dept. requested mutual aid from allied law enforcement agencies in Santa Clara and San Mateo Counties. There were 300 officers assigned and I was one of them, patrolling my old downtown beat, this time with other officers from San Mateo County.

The expected large crowd did show up, an estimated 40,000 people. For the most part, the crowd did not create a lot of police problems, and most people had fun. I was glad to have been part of the victory celebration and meet some of the Brazilian fans. Brazil won the World Cup at the Rose Bowl in Pasadena, beating Italy 3-2 in a tense penalty shootout, the first World Cup final to be decided on penalties.

The crazy high-speed pursuit

One afternoon, county radio put out a broadcast of a vehicle pursuit. Broadmoor police, the only police district in California, were chasing a car associated with an assault with a deadly weapon. County radio soon put out an update that the suspect vehicle was entering south 101 from Brisbane.

Dave Chetcuti and I were at the station. I was the sergeant. I asked him if he wanted to head in the direction of the pursuit. He said he did. Dave jumped into my patrol car and we drove to El Camino and 380. We figured there were two ways we could get in on the chase.

- ▶ *If the suspect vehicle continued south on 101.*
- ▶ *If it drove west on 380 towards 280.*

Keep in mind we had no business getting involved in the chase at all, but Dave and I were in the mood for some excitement.

A Brisbane police unit put out over the radio that the suspect vehicle was passing 380 and continuing south on 101 at 100 plus mph. I drove onto east 380 and quickly entered the on-ramp to south 101.

We found ourselves paralleling the suspect vehicle at 110 mph. The woman passenger in the right front seat was frantically waving at us with both hands. We suddenly found ourselves in the lead position directly behind the suspect vehicle. That is a bad position. We did not want to be there for fear of being identified.

The Brisbane unit got back on the radio and said there was a unit in front of him. County radio requested the lead unit to identify themselves.

Again, because we really should not be involved in the pursuit at all, Dave reluctantly got on the radio and said, "29 SAM 1 is the lead vehicle." That was my call sign, so everybody knew it was me. Then the suspect vehicle began passing traffic on the right shoulder, seriously endangering other drivers.

We should have stopped the pursuit

Shortly thereafter Dave told county radio that we would stop the pursuit. I turned off the siren, but we still trailed the suspect vehicle at about 100 mph. Dave and I really did not want the suspects to get away. Letting them escape would have been the correct decision, particularly since we should have never engaged in the pursuit to begin with.

A large plume of smoke came out of the suspect vehicle's engine compartment as it approached the Poplar Ave. exit. Dave told county radio what we just saw and that the suspect vehicle was exiting 101 at Poplar Ave. in San Mateo.

The vehicle drove behind an apartment complex at less than five mph. The driver started to open the door while the vehicle was still moving. It was obvious he was going to run, or, as we refer to it in the profession, take foot bail. I hit the driver's door with the push bars on the front of the patrol car and forced it all the way forward so it smashed against the left front fender.

The driver got out of the vehicle, jumped on the hood of the patrol car and began running towards a baseball field where a game was being played. Everyone at the game saw me running after the suspect. It was apparent I wasn't going to catch him.

I yelled at the players, "Get him, get him." Several of them picked up baseball bats and started chasing the suspect. He was now in deep left field. As he was climbing the fence, the players were trying to hit his feet. Once the suspect reached the top of the fence, he fell off and landed on the sidewalk.

A San Mateo police officer quickly took him into custody. While all this was going on, Dave arrested the woman passenger.

Go back? We were never there!

I checked the patrol car for damage when I got back and luckily didn't see any. I told Dave we should leave and we started driving away. But then suddenly Dave said, "We have to go back." I joking replied; "Go back? We were never there!" Dave said his handcuffs were on the female passenger and he wanted them back, so we returned to the scene. After Dave traded out his handcuffs, we headed back to Millbrae where we belonged. We were happy. We got our excitement fix for the day!

66 felony counts of child molestation

In April, 1994, Detective Max Bosel, who would go on to become chief of police in Mountain View, just down 101, and I were called upon to investigate a case of child molestation. We discovered a mother who was pimping out her daughters, ages 11 and 13, in exchange for money. She used the cash to buy crack cocaine.

A 55-year-old man who lived in the same complex brought the girls into his apartment where they watched pornographic movies and had sex. The mother, who admitted to the crime, was convicted of prostituting children under 16. She received a prison sentence of 16 years.

We identified 13 other victims, girls ranging in ages from eight to 13. They all lived in the same neighborhood.

The man was convicted of 66 felony counts of child molestation involving oral copulation and sexual intercourse with children under 16. He was sentenced to 80 years in prison. I think the prosecutor in the case said it best, "With such a lengthy sentence, hopefully this extremely dangerous predator will never have the opportunity to molest children any more."

Four pipe bombs and a large quantity of meth

In April, 1996, Dave and I responded to a family disturbance at a house. I saw a pipe bomb on a shelf in one of the bedrooms. It was about nine inches long, capped on each end, with a three-inch fuse protruding from one end.

At first the occupants said they didn't know anything about the pipe bomb. After they consented to a further search, Dave and I found three more. The San Mateo County Sheriff's Office bomb squad removed the bombs.

We also found a shotgun and two handguns, one of them loaded. Dave found a safe in a bedroom and got permission to look inside. The occupant even voluntarily unlocked the safe for him. Dave located a large quantity of meth, a set of scales, and records of narcotics sales.

We found cars and an abundance of vehicle parts. One of the cars was reported stolen out of San Francisco. The county Vehicle

Theft Task Force took possession of the stolen car and the vehicle parts for further investigation. The occupants, who were not getting along, were booked into jail on a variety of felony charges.

An egregious crime and an evil act

In January, 1996, I was called to assist the Hillsborough Police Dept. with the kidnapping for ransom of a 10-year-old girl in accordance with the San Mateo County child abduction protocol. Two men grabbed her while she was walking home from school.

The suspects demanded $800,000 in ransom. The victim's parents were away in Taiwan at the time of the kidnapping. The victim was released 12 hours later, and the ransom was never paid.

The very wealthy town of Hillsborough, where homes sell for many millions of dollars, is near the center of the county. I helped, along with the FBI, to develop a telephone link analysis showing when and where the suspect made calls to the victim's family. Analysts derived other investigative leads from the link chart.

Late in 2017, the suspect, Kevin Lin, applied to renew his visa to stay in the country, triggering an identity check which revealed that he had an active arrest warrant from the Hillsborough police. He was taken into custody on the warrant.

The same year, a San Mateo County Superior Court judge sentenced the 69-year-old Lin to seven years to life in prison for the kidnapping. Authorities said Lin went into hiding until his arrest.

A jury later convicted him. San Mateo County prosecutors called it "justice delayed, but not denied." The judge said while the sentence was mandatory, he "would have imposed it anyway because he found the kidnapping to be an egregious crime and it was an evil act," county District Attorney Stephen Wagstaffe in a press interview.

Openly carrying machetes on their belts

Here is the story of the outlaw motorcycle gang violence that wasn't. The site is the Clarion and Westin Hotels in Millbrae. More than 1,000 members of the Hells Angels attended that convention on the weekend of May 13 and 14, 2000.

I was the incident commander. Intelligence reports from the FBI and the California Dept. of Justice had given us great concern.

Many of the Hells Angels were openly carrying machetes on their belts. A Hells Angels bigwig wanted members of other clubs to join his gang in an action called patching over.

We were under a county-wide tactical alert for the whole weekend. Officers from throughout the county were assigned to the hotels around the clock.

On Sunday afternoon, about 50 members of the notorious Mongols motorcycle gang showed up unexpectedly and congregated in the lobby of the Clarion Hotel. The Hells Angels and the Mongols, who are from southern California, are arch enemies and have a history of violence against each other.

The tension in the air was high when the Mongols were in the hotel. In a military manner, the Mongols lined up around the inside perimeter of the lobby. Fortunately, after being in the hotel for about an hour, the Mongols left without incident. This was unlike what happened at the Harris Casino and Hotel in Laughlin, Nevada in 2002, where a brawl broke out between the Mongols and the Hells Angels and several members were shot.

Dave's surreal on-duty murder

On April 25, 1998, I was off duty, working out in the gym at the Coast Guard Air Station located behind the nearby San Francisco International Airport. Two San Francisco police officers were working out with me. Our radios were on the weight bench. A call came over the police radio of "officer down" at 101 and Millbrae Ave.

I responded to the scene in my own car and found Millbrae Officer Dave Chetcuti dead, lying on the asphalt. No one else was around. Dave had been shot multiple times, three times in the face. I saw large holes in the asphalt around Dave's body as well as spent casings from his .45 caliber handgun and the suspect's rifle.

"If that had been me, I would have wanted you to be first on scene," said retired Mountain View Police Chief Max Bosel years later, "I'm sure Dave looked down from heaven and sighed a breath of relief that someone he respected and loved was there to look after him."

Everything became surreal.

A South San Francisco police officer arrived on scene, followed by an ambulance. He told me police were pursuing the suspect onto the San Mateo-Hayward Bridge. While in complete shock, I went to the station and put my uniform on.

I assisted the lone dispatcher with taking a large volume of phone calls. Many calls were from the press. Many other calls were from members of the law enforcement community asking who the fallen officer was and hoping to get any details about the murder.

One caller reported she was driving south on 101 and saw an officer getting shot. She thought perhaps a movie was being filmed. I told her it wasn't a movie at all and I needed all her contact information because she had witnessed Dave's murder. The phone calls kept pouring in.

Dave was shot and killed when he responded to back up a San Bruno police officer who had a suspect point a rifle at him. The suspect was seen driving on San Bruno Ave. and El Camino with expired registration tabs. The suspect was pulled over on south 101 and Millbrae Ave. As the officer approached the suspect's car, the suspect stepped out of his car and pointed a rifle at him.

The officer radioed for assistance and was able to escape injury by diving into a nearby canal for cover and concealment.

Dave, a motorcycle officer, was the first responding officer on scene. As Dave rode up and got off his motorcycle, the suspect opened fire, striking Dave several times. Dave returned fire, emptying his magazine and hitting the suspect once. One of Dave's .45 caliber bullets grazed the suspect's abdomen, went in and out of one pocket, through the zipper on his jacket and came to rest inside the other jacket pocket. What are the chances?

Once he had killed Dave, the suspect then stole his handgun, got back in his car and fled south on 101. A vehicle pursuit ended when the suspect stopped on the eastern end of the bridge.

The suspect stepped out of the vehicle holding the rifle he shot Dave with as well as the handgun he stole from Dave. He also had three pipe bombs strapped around his chest. One of Dave's bullets was recovered only inches from these bombs. During the high-risk stop, the suspect complied with the officers' verbal commands and was taken into custody. The San Mateo County Sheriff's Office bomb squad secured the bombs.

Commanding the funeral honor guard

I had the privilege of commanding the honor guard for Dave's funeral. I was overwhelmed by the amount of community support that was shown to Dave, his family, and the department.

I was pleased to see people standing along El Camino Real for miles. People were getting out of their cars to show their respect as the motorcade and lengthy procession traveled to Holy Cross Cemetery in Colma. These community members realized the significance of the murder of a police officer.

A great many motorcycle police officers attended Dave's funeral.

Dave's murder was a defining moment in my life. I realized how fragile life is, and it reminded me how being a cop could turn deadly serious in just a split second.

Broadmoor Officer Joe Sheridan, attired in Scottish regalia including a kilt, played the bagpipes at Dave's funeral at the cemetery. Joe is now a sergeant with the San Mateo County Sheriff's Office.

I truly feel most people understand that Dave was not killed because of who he was as an individual, but rather for what he represented. He stood for what was good in the world and was so dedicated that he laid down his life for his strong belief and steadfast devotion to duty.

Nearly everyone lined up along El Camino who were paying their respects were keenly aware Dave would make the ultimate sacrifice for each of them, anytime, anywhere. I truly hope I will be able to make the cut and see Dave again.

The suspect, Marvin Patrick Sullivan, Jr., was found to be unable to aid in his own defense and deemed incompetent to stand trial. He remains confined in Napa State Hospital.

What I learned from Dave's murder

Here is what I learned from this tragedy. I offer this advice:

► *Forget all the bickering and arguing. Appreciate each other every day. If a tragedy like this happens, you'll regret that the last memory you have of a person who died was an argument with you. This really makes it clear that you shouldn't sweat the small stuff.*

► *Use sound police tactics, even on a quiet Saturday morning. Pay attention to officer safety. Stay alert, don't drop your guard, use cover and concealment where possible, take your range and defensive tactics training seriously.*

► *There will be plenty of people out there willing to help you early on. It's wise to take most of them up on their offer. People want to help you organize services; allied officers want to help work your streets; people in the community want to help by bringing food to the police station. Let them. The worst thing you can do is to refuse help.*

Dave lived in Millbrae with his wife, Gail, and their three sons. In 2000, the Millbrae Community Room was dedicated to Dave. It is now known as the Officer David Chetcuti Community Room and the stretch of 101 where Dave was killed is now called the Officer David Chetcuti Memorial Highway. In honor of Dave, to this day, an American flag flies at the place where he was murdered.

Officer Dave Chetcuti
Memorial Highway

Dave and I were not only work partners, but also good friends. Before he became a full-time officer, he was a Millbrae reserve officer. We often rode together on Fridays. I was one of his training officers, although he did not need a lot of training. He had a lot of the natural ability, maturity, and excellent street instincts necessary for being a high-speed police officer. It's hard, if not impossible, to train for great street instincts. It's almost like either you have them or you don't.

After Dave was murdered, Millbrae police installed a police chaplain to support police employees emotionally and spiritually. The chaplain provides appropriate and confidential assistance, advice, comfort, counseling, and referrals to those employees in need. This trust was never violated. I believe chaplains have a positive role in most first-responder organizations.

My mentor changed the CHP and helped establish POBOR

When I was about 10, I met Edward Maghakian, one of my father's fellow CHP officers. Ed was a three-time president of the California Association of Highway Patrolmen, formed in 1920, and a longtime board member. He taught me a great deal and was one of my most important mentors.

Ed was instrumental in transforming the CAHP from a fraternal organization into a labor organization. Before that, officers had to buy their own guns and safety equipment such as rain gear and flashlights.

As if that weren't enough, in the mid-1970s, he also was important in establishing the California Peace Officers' Bill of Rights, called POBOR. He represented the CHP association and worked with other large law enforcement labor organization in the state, including the Los Angeles Police Protective League.

POBOR protects public safety officers when they face internal investigations. It defines clear protections for their personnel records, privacy issues, interrogation tactics, searches, and situations in which interrogation focuses on matters that are likely to result in punishment. Officers have the right to have a representative of their choice with them at all times during the interrogation.

California police officers enjoy these due-process rights to this day. Ed was also appointed to the California Peace Officer's Standard and Training Commission by two-term Governor George Deukmejian Jr. Ed served on the commission for eight years. He left as chair.

Compromise and continuous improvement

Ed taught me about the art of compromise and the importance of continuous improvement. I found these principles useful when I was president of Millbrae Police Officers' Assn. during contract negotiations with the City of Millbrae. Ed also taught me the importance of establishing positive relationships with management to improve and resolve issues of common interest.

Ed practices Buddhism, and he has helped me to look at events with a different perspective. For example, it is never the event that matters, it is how we choose to react to the event that matters. I believe that the study of Buddhism has made me calmer and has helped me with dealing with the wide variety of situations cops are called upon to resolve. I feel my personal life has benefited from this new way of thinking.

FBI National Academy and Compstat

In 2000, I attended the 200th session of the FBI's National Academy at Quantico, Virginia. It is a professional course of study for United States and international law enforcement managers nominated by their agency heads because of demonstrated leadership qualities.

The 10-week program teaches law, intelligence theory, networking, leadership science, behavioral science, law enforcement communication, and forensic science to improve the administration of justice in police departments and agencies in the United States and abroad. It aims to raise law enforcement standards, knowledge, and cooperation worldwide.

Louis Freeh, the FBI director at the time, ran with us one morning. U.S. Attorney General Janet Reno presented me with my diploma. My only legacy at the FBI Academy is my name on a plaque with four other students who swam 25 miles or more while at the academy.

National Academy students from the New York Police Dept. typically host a weekend trip to New York. Only 150 students, chosen by lottery, can attend. I was one of the lucky ones. We got on two charter buses and headed to the Big Apple. We had dinner in Little Italy, went on a tour of the harbor in a New York Fire Dept. boat, visited Saint Patrick's Cathedral, and received an early morning Compstat briefing by a deputy commissioner at One Police Plaza.

NYPD created Compstat, or computerized statistics, in 1995. The system is credited with lowering the crime rate in the city by analyzing statistics and crime trends. Compstat is now used successfully by law enforcement agencies around the world.

The department's top leaders convene weekly Compstat meetings. Precinct commanders are held accountable for reducing crime in their respective parts of the city. My NYPD classmates said that the brass would throw softball questions at the precinct commanders they liked and hardball questions at those they didn't like.

During our free time, a classmate and I toured the World Trade Center. We spent hours on the observation deck taking in the majestic view.

My mother self-medicated with meth

In addition to my late brother, Jason, I have two younger sisters, Carolyn and Tami. Our biological mother was diagnosed with bipolar depression in her mid-twenties.

Tami was six years old and I was nine when a neighbor called the police because our mother left us home alone. We were placed in a children's shelter. Carolyn was not home at the time and stayed with our mother in some hippie commune in the Santa Cruz mountains. We were reunited when our father took custody of the three of us. We lost contact with our mother.

My sisters and I started corresponding with our mother in 1998. It was obvious she wasn't doing well. We traveled to El Cajon down near San Diego and found her at a seedy hotel with a woman friend. We could see that our mother was self-medicating with methamphetamines. It was very difficult to see her in such a terrible way. We took her shopping at a nearby Target store for some basic necessities, out to lunch, and gave her money.

She was dealt a bad hand. My sisters and I felt a great deal of sympathy for her. I was reminded that anyone could find themselves in a similar plight. No one is above becoming a drug user or homeless. I am reminded of a 1553 quote by John Bradford "There but for the grace of God go I."

This experience with my mother had a profound effect on my duties as a police officer and a human being. When I encountered people who are on drugs, homeless, without money, or all these severe difficulties, I thought that they could be my mother. My perspective changed. I became more compassionate and less judgmental. Ultimately, our mother found a government-subsidized apartment and started receiving Social Security checks for her mental illness.

Chapter 4
United States Coast Guard

Not only was I fascinated with police work as a teenager, I was also interested in the military. If I hadn't been hired by the Los Gatos police right out of high school, I planned to enlist in the Army and become a military police officer. I figured that the experience of being in the Army and being trained as an MP would help with securing a civilian police officer position after I was discharged. This plan worked well for my father.

U.S. COAST GUARD TRAINING CENTER CAPE MAY N.J.
MARTIP   02 - 97
EMC   TURLINGTON

My graduating class from the U.S Coast Guard BasicTraining.

12-hour police shifts propel me into the Coast Guard Reserve

Millbrae police went to 12-hour patrol shifts in 1996. Officers had Thursdays, Fridays, and Saturdays as well as every other Wednesday off. This meant four days off every other week. I didn't know what to do with all the time off. Then it hit me.

The Coast Guard Reserve had a direct-entry petty officer program for those with a college degree. I was one year under the age limit of 35, so I seized the opportunity. One drill weekend a month and two weeks of annual training in the summer would be perfect for helping to fill both the void created by the 12-hour schedule and my lifelong aspiration to be part of the military.

I enlisted in the Coast Guard as a petty officer third class with the rate of Coast Guard Investigative Service special agent. In February, 1997, I shipped off to Cape May, New Jersey, for basic training.

I was assigned to Coast Guard Island in Alameda, California, and processed into my new unit. Everything was going well as a reserve special agent, and then our country was attacked by terrorists.

My son Jeffrey and me in a Coast Guard vessel.

One of the Coast Guard's first sea marshals

Shortly after Sept. 11, 2001, I received active-duty orders. I would become one of the Coast Guard's first sea marshals. Other active-duty Coast Guard Investigative Services agents and a long list of special agents from a variety of federal agencies became air marshals.

The duties of a sea marshal were to secure the bridge and engine rooms on all ships entering and leaving the San Francisco Bay.

We worked alongside the San Francisco bar pilots, the only captains allowed to sail large ships in and out of the Bay. They have the technical knowledge to understand the intricacies and tide patterns unique to the Bay. When the fog is heavy, it is not uncommon for bar pilots to sail some of the largest ships in the world under the Golden Gate Bridge without ever seeing the bridge.

Sea marshals were tasked with preventing terrorists from taking control of ships and running them into the Golden Gate Bridge, some other vessel, a pier, or other target of opportunity. We realized that even crew members could support Al Qaeda, or even be affiliated with that terrorist organization. The ships included oil tankers, container ships, cruise ships, and bulk carriers from all over the world. It was interesting meeting and interacting with the various crew members of a variety of nationalities.

When we sailed out of San Francisco, Oakland, Sacramento, or Stockton, we would go 13 miles west of the Golden Gate Bridge to the site of the San Francisco sea buoy and the pilot station. The station is a bar pilot boat.

Climbing Jacob's ridiculously dangerous ladder

We climbed off ships using a wood and rope Jacob's ladder and jumped onto the pilot boat, which was paralleling the ship at the same speed. This was a very dangerous maneuver and often done at night. Falling into the Pacific Ocean outright or getting crushed between our boat and the pilot boat and then falling into the ocean was always a real possibility.

When a ship was entering the Bay, the pilot boat would again parallel the ship and we would jump off the pilot boat and onto the side of the ship that had yet another Jacob's ladder hanging off the side. We climbed up and boarded the vessel. We would then either go to the bridge or the engine room to secure it from the bad guys.

The Sea Marshals program, which started in the San Francisco Bay, expanded around the country to the ports of Los Angeles, Long Beach, and San Diego, among others. A large team of mobilized reservists, mostly civilian police officers, served in major sea ports along the eastern seaboard as well. I was a sea marshal for six months. I will always reflect on it as a privilege to serve my country, although in a very small way, right after our homeland was attacked.

Terrorist attacks on ocean vessels have occurred before. One notable example is the hijacking of the cruise ship Achille Lauro. Four men representing the Palestinian Liberation Front hijacked the vessel off the coast of Egypt, on Oct. 7, 1995, as she was sailing from Alexandria, Egypt to Ashdod, Israel.

The idea of somebody using a ship itself as a weapon was never given a great deal of thought. That changed on 9/11.

Suddenly, previously harmless vessels were seen as weapons in the waiting. Sea marshals mirrored what air marshals were doing on airliners. Air marshals were covert, operating in plain clothes. Sea marshals were overt, as we wore uniforms.

Coast Guard screens crew, manifest, cargo

Before vessels entered the San Francisco Bay, the Coast Guard screened the crew manifest, cargo, and about 20 other variables. All ships must now notify the Coast Guard 96 hours before entering any U.S. port to allow time for these security checks and analyses. This began an era where the once unimaginable now seemed possible. We know the 9/11 terrorist attacks occurred, in part, due to a breakdown of imagination.

I was called again to active duty in March, 2003, when the United States and its allies invaded Iraq. I was on a task force that conducted background checks on mariners who were issued licenses by the Coast Guard and had failed to disclose felony convictions on their applications.

It was about this time the Coast Guard decided to make most of the active-duty agents warrant officers, but, for the most part, expressed no interest with doing the same for reserve agents. I really wanted to be a warrant officer and found out that the Army Criminal Investigative Division had a career track for promoting enlisted reserve agents to warrant officers.

A friend who was a fellow San Jose police cadet introduced me to a reserve unit on the Oakland Army Base. My friend Steven Gutierrez was a former commander of the unit. He retired from the San Jose Police Dept. as a sergeant and from the Army as lieutenant colonel.

Chapter 5

United States Army

380th Military Police Detachment (CID).

After seven and a half years in the Coast Guard, I switched branches and enlisted in the Army at the Military Entrance Processing Center at Moffett Field down the freeway in Mountain View.

Coast Guard blue to Army green

The transition seemed like it was going to be fairly smooth until the recruiter said I would not be able to carry my Coast Guard rank of E-6 over to the Army. I would have to drop down to E-5. The recruiter said it would be like taking one step backwards to take two steps forward. The proposal did not appeal to me.

I told the recruiter I would have to think about it and left. While I drove home, the recruiter called my cell phone and said I would be able to keep my E-6 rank.

I turned the car around and returned to MEPS. I signed the contract and was attached to the 380th Military Police Detachment at the Oakland Army Base. My goal was to become a chief warrant officer.

B.U.M.-blame, understand, and minimize

Joining the Army would turn out to be one of the best career decisions I ever made. In May, 2006, I received active-duty orders to deploy to the Middle East. Before I went overseas, I had to complete the five-and-a-half-month CID special agent course at Fort Leonard Wood in Missouri, home of the Army's military police school, which is very much like the police academy.

The school emphasized conducting thorough crime scene examinations and intensely emphasized interview and interrogation techniques, along with blood-spatter evidence, and collecting and preserving DNA evidence. I had been a police officer for 15 years, and the CID training made me a more knowledgeable and detail-oriented cop.

Agents learned ways to develop rapport to ultimately get to the truth when they conducted subject interviews. Some of the rapport-building themes were blaming someone or something else for what happened, understanding why a subject did what he or she did, and minimizing the subject's action. The acronym is B.U.M.: blame, understand, and minimize.

Successful interviewing and interrogating are really art. Some cops or agents have an almost natural ability to draw the truth out of people. Army CID made obtaining subject confessions a high priority and invested in the training to allow agents to be effective interviewers with the goal of seeking the truth. Days started out at 5 a.m. with organized physical training, followed by reporting to the classroom no later than 8 a.m.

My uniform insignias.

Deployed to Iraq, the wrong country

When I graduated, I joined 10 other apprentice agents to travel to Fort Campbell, Kentucky, our mobilization station, and link up with our active-duty counterparts. Fort Campbell is the home of the legendary 101st Airborne Division, known as the Screaming Eagles.

We had two months of pre-deployment training consisting of convoy operations, advanced first aid, detection of improvised explosive devices, and a lot of range or trigger time with the M-4 rifle.

In November, 2006, my new unit, comprised of reserve and active duty agents, formed the 280th Military Police Detachment, falling under the 22nd Military Police Battalion.

A chartered bus took us to Pope Air Force Base in North Carolina. We boarded a civilian commercial jetliner and flew to Bangor, Maine; for refueling and Shannon, Ireland; for more refueling.

In Al-Faw Palace in Baghdad.

After 12 hours of flying, we landed at Kuwait City International Airport. We then dispersed to our respective offices scattered throughout Iraq and Kuwait. Our battalion headquarters was in Baghdad, Iraq.

At first, I was assigned to Camp Buehring, Kuwait, close to Iraq's southern border. It was the last stop for troops heading to Iraq. Troops wouldn't spend more than a week there.

The arms holding the swords are supposed to be Saddam Hussein's.

The driver and the ground guide were best friends

An infantry unit composed of armored personnel carriers called Bradley Fighting Vehicles arrived at the camp. Infantry would participate in training primarily consisting of going to the range and qualifying with various weapon systems.

One afternoon we responded to a fatal collision.

A soldier was acting as a ground guide, giving hand signals to the driver of a Bradley parked close behind another Bradley. The ground guide was standing in between the stopped Bradley and the moving Bradley.

As the moving Bradley came to a stop, it suddenly lurched forward, crushing the ground guide in half. What made the tragedy even worse was the fact that the driver of the Bradley and the ground guide were best friends. The dead soldier was going to be the driver's best man at his wedding after their deployment.

A week after we investigated the Bradley fatality, country singer Carrie Underwood came to Camp Buehring on a USO tour. I was assigned to her protection detail. Ms. Underwood's support for the troops was sincere and she put on a great show for the service members who were on their way to Iraq.

With Carrie Underwood after her USO concert.

In 2005, she became the season four winner of American Idol. At the time, I wasn't too familiar with her. However, I have since become a big and loyal fan. I cherish the picture of us together.

Iraq had become the proverbial hole

President George W. Bush signed a controversial order in January, 2007, authorizing thousands of additional troops into Iraq to secure neighborhoods and reduce hostilities. Camp Buehring suddenly became an even busier place with little room to temporarily house the troop surge. The lines for the mess halls were incredibly long.

The troop surge reminds me of a quote by Will Rogers, "When you find yourself in a hole, quit digging." In other words, you can dig yourself into a hole but you can't dig yourself out of a hole. Iraq had become the proverbial hole.

I was assigned to the Protective Services Detail for Adm. Edmund Giambastiani, vice chairman of the Joint Chiefs of Staff. The detail was stationed primarily at the Victory Base Complex in Baghdad; the complex contained Camp Victory, Camp Liberty, and the Baghdad International Airport, formerly the Saddam Hussein International Airport.

We spent the better part of a day running the quickest routes and alternate routes leading to the Combat Support Hospital in Baghdad to prepare for the admiral's arrival. The hospital was then taking in 10 to 20 trauma cases a day.

With Agent Jeremy Reeves. Notice the black smoke in the background from an exploding car.

We also went into the hospital to become familiar with the layout, particularly the emergency room. We confirmed that the ER had enough of the admiral's blood type in the event he became seriously wounded.

The admiral spent most of his time at the Al-Faw Palace, the headquarters of the Multi-National Corps-Iraq. Saddam Hussein spent a lot of his time at the same palace before the United States and allied forces invaded.

Occasionally, the admiral had to leave the Victory Base Complex for meetings at the United States Embassy in the Green Zone, a heavily guarded five-mile plus area in central Baghdad housing international coalition forces and government officials.

A rocket landed about 20 yards from us

One morning other members of the Admiral's protection detail and I convoyed from the complex to the Green Zone. Members of the Kentucky Army National Guard ran the convoy. The Guard members were in up-armored Humvees. They were a bunch of good old boys and enjoyable to work with.

We took Route Irish to the Green Zone. I found out later that Route Irish was active with improvised explosive devices and sniper fire. We were the last vehicle in a Chevrolet Suburban with a bullet-proof windshield and side-passenger windows. We were assigned to the advance team, arranging for the admiral to arrive by helicopter in the afternoon.

Heading into the Green Zone.

A rocket landed about 20 yards from us just before we entered the checkpoint at the Green Zone. Several service members playing volleyball were hit by shrapnel and fell to the ground. The blast shattered the Suburban's far-back, right-side window.

A second rocket landed in the same spot as the first rocket, again hitting the volleyball players with even more shrapnel. The second rocket shattered our far-left, rear window. We were already wearing ballistic vests, but not our Kevlar helmets. We put them on and ran inside a nearby concrete bunker until the "take cover" siren ended.

Most of the volleyball players were seriously injured, but luckily no one died, although one player lost his lower leg. The explosion made my ears ring for days. I lost my hearing. We were very lucky one of the rockets didn't land on top of the Suburban.

One of my main responsibilities was to be at the gym every day at 5 a.m. and get on a stationary bike. When the admiral entered the gym, I got off the bike and the admiral got on it. This guaranteed the admiral would have a bike available and wouldn't have to wait.

The largest prison in the world

I was assigned to Camp Bucca, the CID prison located in Basra in southeast Iraq, in April, 2007. At the time it was the largest prison in the world with 20,000 detainees. The U.S. military took it over in April, 2003 and renamed it after New York City Fire Marshal Ronald Bucca, who died in the 9/11 terrorist attacks. He was the only fire marshal in the history of the FDNY to be killed in the line of duty.

Like Saddam Hussein, most of the detainees were Sunni. This region of Iraq was populated by Shia. Even if a Sunni detainee were to escape from Camp Bucca, he would be in danger from the local Shias.

Extremist organizations from Afghanistan, not Iraq

My fellow soldiers agreed that the United States and allies were in Iraq only to stop the Iraqis from killing each other. Why else would the U.S. invade a sovereign country?

At this point, the belief that Iraq had weapons of mass destruction, justifying our invasion of the country, had been completely debunked. The enemies who attacked the United States of America on 9/11 were members of Al-Qaeda and the Taliban. These extremist organizations were clearly from Afghanistan, not Iraq. As soldiers we are duty-bound to follow orders, so we went to Iraq, the wrong country.

One morning a prison detainee was found beaten to death. Through an interpreter, I interviewed every detainee in the compound. They all denied any knowledge of the murder. In reality, everyone knew the victim and why he was killed. Just like the unwritten rule in San Mateo County jail, "snitches get stitches," applied to the largest prison in the world.

I was home on leave for two weeks, when, on June 9, 2007, six detainees were killed and 68 wounded, including one Iraqi corrections officer who was hurt when a rocket struck Compound 8. This was a major international news story. I missed being there by a week.

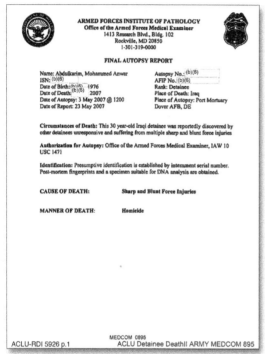

Even within the Sunnis, there were two rival sects, Wahhabi Islam and Hanbali Islam. Even though they are both Sunni, it was difficult for them to coexist. This resulted in frequent detainee-on-detainee violence. It reminded me of the Surenos and Nortenos gangs in the San Mateo County jail.

While at Bagram Air Base CID office, 30 miles north of Kabul, Afghanistan, I was on a protective detail for the chairman of the Joint Chiefs of Staff, Gen. Peter Pace. He was nice enough to give me and the other agents on the detail one of his personal challenge coins.

My official U.S. Army portrait.

Possibly trading jet fuel for alcohol in Afghanistan

While still in Afghanistan, I was assigned to a case of an Army staff sergeant who was reportedly trading jet fuel for alcohol. The sergeant was the non-commissioned officer in charge of a fuel point at a forward operating base.

I'm the one on the left.

The investigation was to determine if the staff sergeant was accepting alcohol from Afghan nationals who were supposed to deliver JP-8 jet fuel to the base, but never actually did. These fuel points were used to refuel helicopters in support of the war effort.

Allegedly, the staff sergeant would sign receipts as if hundreds of gallons of fuel were delivered to the base. Actually, the Afghani truck drivers would leave the base with a fuel truck still full of fuel, minus several bottles of alcohol.

An audit of the fuel point revealed that thousands of gallons of fuel were diverted at a loss to the government of about $200,000. More importantly, it was possible that the truck drivers were giving the fuel to the Taliban. If this was proven, the staff sergeant could be charged with aiding the enemy, a capital offense. The Army has not imposed the death penalty in 60 years.

The case came to CID's attention when one of the privates at the base had a falling out with the staff sergeant and notified CID of his concerns. I left Afghanistan before this case was resolved.

Challenge coins. Top row: Admiral Edmund Giambastiani, General James Cartwright, Joint Chiefs of Staff. Middle row: Robert M. Gates, Secretary of Defense, General Mark A. Milley, Admiral Mike Mullen. Bottom row: General Raymond Odierno, General Peter Pace.

Joint Chiefs of Staff

The Joint Chiefs of Staff is a panel of high-ranking U.S. military officers who advise the president of the United States and other civilian leaders on military issues.

The Joint Chiefs of Staff consist of the Chairman, the Vice Chairman, the Chief of Staff of the Army, the Chief of Naval Operations, the Chief of Staff of the Air Force, the Commandant of the Marine Corps, the Chief of the National Guard Bureau, and the Chief of Space Operations.

These coins represent the individual military leaders the U.S. Army Protective Service Battalion served.

Protecting the top, top, top brass

In preparation for an upcoming unit mobilization to support the 701st Protective Services Battalion at Fort Belvoir, Virginia, I attended a three-week protective services training course in Missouri. It covered mission planning and coordination, protective services in a hostile fire zone, special weapons training, evasive driving, and motorcade operations. A comprehensive four-day practical exercise ended the training.

In August 2010, my unit was attached to the 701st Personnel Services Branch. The mission was to provide worldwide protection to the top 11 Dept. of Defense officials, starting with the Secretary of Defense.

I was assigned to the Office of the Joint Chiefs detachment. Adm. Mike Mullen was the chairman of the joint chiefs and Gen. James Cartwright was the vice chairman. We provided Secret Service-type protection around the clock and around the world. The detachment had two teams, a metro team and a travel team.

Agents on the metro team would typically pick up the admiral or general at 5 a.m. at their quarters or residence. The principal would ride in the limousine, driven by an agent. A chase vehicle followed it. The chase car had two agents in it, the driver and the shift leader, who was armed with a handgun and a submachine gun. The principal's personal security officer would be in the limo.

We would motorcade to the Pentagon. From there we would take our principals to the White House, the Central Intelligence

Agency headquarters in Mclean, Virginia; Congress; Bethesda Naval Medical Center in Maryland; or Walter Reed National Military Medical Center, also in Bethesda. We drove them to various speaking engagements around the Beltway or in the capitol region.

Visiting the amputee ward

During one of the trips to Walter Reed, we visited the amputee ward. I saw three quadruple amputee service members. I was not prepared for that. Whenever I think I am having a bad day, I think of the sacrifice these wounded warriors made. They survived because of our advancements in treating traumatic injuries. I am pretty sure that they would have perished if they were injured during Vietnam or previous wars.

Adm. Mullen and Gen. Cartwright were committed to visiting wounded warriors whose lives were upended in the wars at the military hospitals.

One afternoon, I was on Gen. Cartwright's detail when he visited Section 60 in the sacred Arlington National Cemetery, the 14-acre graveyard where more than 800 veterans from Iraq and Afghanistan wars are buried. This made for a solemn afternoon.

As part of the advance travel team for Adm. Mullen, I went to Riyadh, Saudi Arabia for two weeks. With only a few exceptions, women were still not allowed to drive there.

The story is that there is no story

Adm. Mullen supported ending the "Don't Ask, Don't Tell" policy, which banned gay men and lesbians from serving openly in the military.

He testified before Congress to repeal the ill-fated policy. He told Congress "Speaking for myself and myself only, it is my personal belief that allowing gays and lesbians to serve openly would be the right thing to do. No matter how I look at the issue, I cannot escape being troubled by the fact that we have in place a policy which forces young men and women to lie about who they are in order to defend their fellow citizens."

President Barack Obama ultimately repealed the policy. Years after the repeal, the story was there was no story. The military adapted to the change without any problems.

Celebrating when SEAL Team Six kills Osama bin Laden

On May 1, 2011, a Sunday, while on the metro team, we picked up Gen. Cartwright from his residence and motorcaded to the White House. We knew Secretary of Defense Robert Gates and Adm. Mullen were either on their way to the White House or already there. This may have been the only Sunday I worked as a metro team member.

It was obvious that something big was occurring, but we had no idea what it was. Late in the evening, we motorcaded Gen. Cartwright back to his residence.

When I got back to my apartment in Alexandria, Va., the breaking news story was that Navy SEAL Team Six had killed Osama bin Laden at his compound in Abbottabad, Pakistan. Once people heard the news, they celebrated in the streets of the District of Columbia and elsewhere. I will always remember where I was when the 10-year hunt ended.

In August 2008, I attended the Warrant Officer Candidate School at Fort Rucker, Alabama. Unlike the police academy where I was the youngest in the class, now as a warrant officer candidate, I was the oldest. I actually had to get an age waiver as the age limit to attend was 45 and I was 46.

Promoted to Chief Warrant Officer 2

After five weeks of intensive academic and physical training, I was appointed to the rank of Warrant Officer 1. Two years later, I was promoted to the commissioned rank of Chief Warrant Officer 2.

After leaving the Protective Services Battalion and back at my reserve unit, I was on protection details with Secretary of Defense Marine Gen. James Mattis. One evening I was assigned to his control room. He had just returned to the hotel after dinner at

George Schultz's house on the Stanford University campus. He thanked us and said he was working us too hard.

I was also on details for Chief of Staff of the Army Gen. Raymond Odierno and with General Mark Milley, now chairman of the Joint Chiefs of Staff.

Investigating widespread recruiting fraud

In September, 2012, I received two-year active duty orders and was attached to Task Force Raptor. My partner, an FBI agent, along with federal agents from around the country, investigated one of the U.S. Army's largest financial scandals, the G-RAP recruitment program.

G-RAP, short for Guard Recruiting Assistance Program, was a financial incentive plan that encouraged Army National Guard members to recruit civilians into the National Guard.

We uncovered a fraudulent kickback scheme. I conducted hundreds of telephone interviews and traveled up and down California interviewing suspects and witnesses.

The scheme started when potential recruits walked into a recruiting office on their own. They were not referred by the recruiter or by a recruiter assistant.

Corrupt recruiters would put their assistant recruiter friends in for the $1,000 referral bonus, and when the recruit shipped out to basic training, the recruiter would put the same friend's name in for an additional $1,000. Often the recruiter and the assistant would split the $2,000, even though the assistant never met or referred the recruit.

Official recruiters are just doing their jobs. But the fraudulent phantom recruiter and assistant were not entitled to any G-RAP bonuses. For dentists and doctors, these bonuses were as high as $75,000.

The potential recruits who just wanted to serve their country with the real possibility of going to war had no idea they were a part of a large recruitment scam. They did not need any additional incentive to join the military.

When I interviewed these recruits, they often told me that they did not know the assistant received G-RAP money for them enlisting.

Despite its success in assisting the National Guard with recruitment, G-RAP was ripe for fraud.

The National Guard's top leadership began receiving allegations of internal fraud associated with the program starting in 2009. One of my cases involved a retired National Guard recruiter who became an assistant. He received $95,000 from G-RAP, the vast majority of that through fraud. I heard reports of assistants receiving over $200,000 by scamming G-RAP.

The G-RAP program lacked anti-fraud measures and was easily taken advantage of by hundreds, possibly thousands, of so-called "recruiters." Soon after the allegations began, hundreds of National Guardsmen were discovered scamming the program and consequently, the taxpayers, out of millions of dollars. An Army Audit Agency estimated a loss of about $50 million and it could be even higher. In May, 2016, the G-Rap program and investigation by Task Force Raptor appeared on the highly regarded television news show *60 Minutes.*

I testified before federal grand juries. This resulted in indictments and federal jury trials in Sacramento and Fresno. Three defendants were convicted of wire fraud. They each received a one-year sentence in federal prison. The Army reserve had the same program, but didn't have the same level of fraud as G-RAP.

Honoring Special Agent Sgt. Joseph Michael Peters

In February, 2015, I attended the Warrant Officer Advance Course in Missouri. Chief Warrant Officers must take the course before they are promoted to Chief Warrant Officer 3.

Our class project was to help the parents of a CID agent killed in Afghanistan.

Special Agent Sgt. Joseph Michael Peters, 24 years old, of the 286th Military Police Detachment in Vicenza, Italy, died from injuries he sustained in a devastating series of blasts from suicide bombs and improvised explosive devices near Kandahar, Afghanistan, while accompanying Army Rangers on a raid on October 6, 2013.

His parents lived in nearby Springfield, Missouri. The class spent a couple of days cleaning their front and back yards, painting parts of the house and general maintenance. We made several trips to the dump. They were very grateful for everything we did to spruce up their house. Afterwards, we all went to the Missouri State Veterans Cemetery in Springfield, where Agent Peters is laid to rest, paying our respects.

Agent Peters was a devoted husband, father, son, brother, and friend. He is survived by his wife, Ashley Peters, and his son, Gabriel Peters, among many other family members.

The huge shoulder patch collection at the Globe and Laurel

Just outside the gates of Marine Corps Base Quantico, in the small town of Triangle, Va., is the Globe and Laurel, a famous restaurant owned by retired Maj. Rick Spooner, U.S. Marine Corps. It opened in 1968.

Students and staff from the FBI Academy, members of the military, members of the Drug Enforcement Agency, among many other government agencies, have made this iconic restaurant a mandatory stop.

It has a large shoulder patch collection. The ceiling is plastered with military, fire services, and law enforcement patches from around the world.

Maj. Spooner is always eager to share his knowledge of Marine Corps history. He grew up in San Francisco and served in three wars: World War II, the Korean War, and the Vietnam War.

Delicious food and even better company

When I was attached to the Army 701st Protective Services Battalion, I spent many of my days off hanging out with Maj. Spooner. We smoked cigars together in the back patio. The food was delicious and the company was even better.

Many notable people with military and law enforcement backgrounds, even both, frequented the restaurant. If you are ever in the District of Columbia, I highly recommend the Globe and Laurel. Maj. Spooner is a great American.

Often referred to as the Tom Clancy of the Marine Corps, Maj. Spooner has written three books.

- ► 2004: ***The Spirit of Semper Fidelis: Reflections from the Bottom of an Old Canteen Cup*** is his memoir as a Marine serving in the Pacific during World War II.
- ► 2011: ***A Marine Anthology: The Spirit of Semper Fidelis a*** historical look at the U. S. Marine Corps through a collection of stories from the Boxer Rebellion to the Battle of Saipan.
- ► 2014: ***The Dragon of Destiny and the Saga of Shanghai Pooley.*** The experiences of iconic Marines are told through Sgt. Paul 'Shanghai' Pooley. Maj. Spooner uses personal experiences and the stories of those Marines he served with during World War II to explain the struggles and triumphs of the combat Marine.

All three of these books have outstanding reviews.

My official portrait from the San Mateo County Sheriff's Office.

The San Mateo County Sheriff's Office has always provided unwavering support to me and every other military reservist in the department. Sheriff Carlos Bolanos allowed me time off to fulfill my military duties. There was never any conflict from the office about allowing reservists to go on military leave, sometimes at very short notice. Not every reservist is the U.S. has this privilege. Sheriff Bolanos received a Patriot Award in 2016 for his efforts from the Employer Support of Guard and Reserve organization.

Chapter 6
San Mateo County Sheriff's Office

I became a deputy sheriff when the San Mateo County Sheriff's Office absorbed the Millbrae police on March 4, 2012.

Millbrae police disband and I become a deputy sheriff

The Millbrae City Council voted to disband its police department and enter into a contract with the sheriff to provide police services to the city, largely because it made financial sense. San Carlos and Half Moon Bay had already done the same. Almost 10 years later, the residents and visitors of Millbrae receive high-quality police services.

My call sign is 2-David-943.

Rival gang members and 'the bucket'

As a new deputy sheriff, my first assignment was in corrections, more commonly referred to as "the bucket." During one of my first days in the jail, I was in a housing unit or pod with my training officer. There are two tiers to a pod, 24 cells per tier, two inmates per cell, and 96 inmates per pod when the bucket is at full capacity. Rival gang members, sex offenders, and high-profile prisoners such as police officers have to be separated from the general population.

Only two deputies are typically assigned to a pod. This high inmate-to-deputy ratio can be challenging and dangerous.

My training officer was teaching me how to manage a pod so that chaos doesn't break out. He told me to pay extra attention when I electronically and remotely unlocked cells when an inmate is leaving his cell or returning to it. If I inadvertently opened a cell with a rival gang member inside, a fight could erupt.

He went into some length explaining the repercussions from opening the wrong door. I knew he was giving me good advice, but thought he was exaggerating a bit to make his point really clear.

Sure enough, the next day a Sureno gang member, those who identify with southern California and wear blue, was returning to the pod after a court appearance. He went up to the second tier and stood in front of his cell to be let in. I mistakenly opened the cell next to where the Sureno was standing.

Without delay, two Norteno gang members, those who identify with northern California and wear red, ran out of their open cell and started beating up the lone Sureno. My training officer and another deputy just happened to be there. I ran up to the second tier and broke up the fight.

My training officer did not exaggerate. What he told me would happen, actually occurred just like he said. From then on, I manually locked and unlocked the cells. This turned out to be a good way to get in some exercise during a 12-hour shift. I had to write a report charging the two Nortenos with assault and battery with gang enhancements.

Catching a Caltrain vandal in San Francisco

One evening we were working at the Caltrain station at Fourth St. and Townsend St. in San Francisco. The sheriff's office is under contract to provide police services for Caltrain, which runs from Gilroy to San Francisco, traveling through Santa Clara, San Mateo and San Francisco Counties.

When the San Francisco Giants and the Golden State Warriors are playing home games, San Mateo County deputy sheriffs are assigned to the station at the end of the line to monitor the passengers getting on and off the trains.

The station agent told us that the inbound train had a passenger who vandalized the train with a Magic Marker and etched the windows with a knife. As soon as the train pulled into the station, the doors opened and a male subject wearing a hoodie started running directly at us while the conductor was yelling, "That's him!"

The suspect ran directly into a deputy and kind of bounced off him. As he ran near me, I grabbed his hoodie, and as he pulled away I ripped the hood off. He continued to run away from us, but we finally wrestled him down to the platform and handcuffed him without further incident. To our surprise, the suspect was only 14. When he was running towards us he could have been 20. We had no idea he was a teenager. We also found a knife on him.

My body camera was knocked off my uniform and slid 30 feet or so down the platform during all the commotion.

Meeting Medal of Honor Recipients

Every September, the Navy SEAL Foundation meets at the Ritz-Carlton Hotel in Half Moon Bay, California, for a golf tournament and other activities.

Capt. Richard Phillips was the guest speaker in 2018. Somali pirates hijacked his ship, the *MV Maersk Alabama*, on April, 8, 2009. One of the three hijackers was armed with an AK-47. Also present were members of SEAL Team Six who rescued him. The ship was en route to Mombasa, Kenya, loaded with relief supplies and food when it was hijacked by pirates in the Indian Ocean off the coast of Mogadishu.

I had the privilege of meeting him and some of the SEALS involved in the dramatic at-sea hostage rescue. The movie *Captain Phillips*, starring Tom Hanks, tells the story of the events leading up to the dramatic hostage rescue of Capt. Phillips and the pirates being simultaneously neutralized by SEAL snipers.

During the Navy SEAL Foundation event, I also had the privilege of meeting three Medal of Honor recipients, all Navy SEALS. They are Lt. Michael E. Thornton, Lt. Thomas Norris, and Master Chief Petty Officer Britt Slabinski

*My father, Richard Grogan, with me and Medal of Honor recipient
Lt. Thomas Norris.*

Lt. Thornton received the medal for his actions while in Vietnam in 1972 during a very protracted firefight, saving the life of a fellow SEAL. The SEAL he saved later received the Medal of Honor for his own actions in an unrelated event. This is the only time this has happened.

Master Chief Petty Officer Slabinski received the medal for his actions during Operation Anaconda in 2002, where he, too, rescued a teammate, Petty Officer 1st Class Neil Roberts.

All three men are truly war heroes who exemplify the very finest and bravest of our nation's military.

My father and I attended another SEAL tribute ceremony in Sept., 2021. Two of the distinguished guests were Thomas Norris and Michael Thornton. Both Norris and Thornton served in Vietnam as Navy SEALS. Each received the medal for rescuing fellow service members under extreme combat conditions.

In 2019, I had the privilege of meeting Thornton and having a picture taken with him. He gave me my most treasured challenge coin. This time my father and I had the privilege of meeting and getting a picture with Norris, who, like Thornton, was wearing his Medal of Honor. Norris said he was just a courier of the medal for previous recipients who were awarded their medals posthumously.

The Medal of Honor is the highest award for valor in action against an enemy force that can be bestowed upon an individual serving in the Armed Services of the United States, according to a fact sheet.

The deed performed must have been one of personal bravery or self-sacrifice so conspicuous as to clearly distinguish the individual above his comrades and must have involved risk of life.

It is the only medal that is worn around the neck, not pinned to the uniform. The medal was first awarded during the Civil War. There are only 103 living recipients of the Medal of Honor.

Norris was very humble. He said what he did in Vietnam was what any SEAL would have done in the same situation. Thornton was awarded the medal, in part, for saving the life of Norris who three years later received the medal for saving the life of Air Force Lt. Colonel Iceal "Gene" Hambleton. Norris' heroic actions were memorialized in a book and documentary movie titled *Bat*21*.

In April, 1972, Norris was one of few remaining SEALS in Vietnam serving with South Vietnam Military with the Naval Advisory Detachment Danang. Aerial combat search and rescue operations failed when Lt. Col. Hambleton was shot down behind enemy lines, leading to the loss of five more aircraft and the death of 11 or more airmen. Two airmen were captured and three more were injured and needed to be rescued.

More than a mile behind enemy lines

Norris was assigned to mount a ground operation to recover Hambleton, Lt. Mark Clark, and Lt. Bruce Walker from behind enemy lines. Assisted by Vietnamese Sea Commando forces, he and Republic of Vietnam Navy Petty Officer Nguyen Van Kiet traveled more than a mile behind enemy lines and successfully rescued two of the downed American aviators. Walker was discovered and killed by the North Vietnamese Army.

At the Ritz-Carlton Hotel in Half Moon Bay with Medal of Honor recipient Lt. Michael Thornton.

Thornton and Norris accompanied a three-man South Vietnamese Navy team on an intelligence-gathering mission in enemy-held territory. The patrol found themselves farther behind enemy lines than they had planned. Continuing on foot, they came under heavy fire from a far larger force and were in danger of being surrounded. While inflicting heavy casualties on the enemy, they headed for the shore, in hopes of escaping by sea.

He found out that Norris had been hit by enemy fire and believed that he was dead. He returned through a hail of fire to Norris' last position and found him severely wounded and unconscious, but alive. Quickly killing two enemy soldiers who approached at that moment, Thornton slung Norris over his shoulder and dashed for life over 400 yards of open beach, returning enemy fire as he ran.

Thornton carried Norris and another wounded comrade out to the South China Sea surf beyond the range of enemy fire. Inflating Norris's life jacket, Thornton kept him afloat and swam for about two hours before being rescued by the South Vietnamese Navy. Norris, who had been shot in the head, later underwent multiple surgeries.

A 10-foot statue depicting Lt. Thornton carrying Lt. Norris on his shoulders is on display at the National Navy UDT-SEAL Museum in Fort Pierce, Florida. "It was the only time this century when one Medal of Honor winner was rescued by a person who would eventually get a Medal of Honor for rescuing him," said Rick Kaiser, executive director of the museum.

Sneaking out of Bethesda Naval Hospital

Close to a year after his heroics in Vietnam, on October 15, 1973, President Richard Nixon awarded Thornton the Medal of Honor at the White House. Lt. Norris was still a patient at nearby Bethesda Naval Hospital. His doctors had forbidden him to go to the ceremony, but Thornton spirited him out the back door of hospital and took him along.

Almost three years later, Norris, himself, received the medal with Thornton looking on. Thornton is the first person in more than a century to receive that honor for saving the life of another Medal of Honor recipient.

Norris applied to the Federal Bureau of Investigation and requested a waiver for his combat disabilities. FBI director William Webster responded, "If you can pass the same test as anybody else applying for this organization, I will waive your disabilities." In Sept. 1979, Norris passed the test and became an FBI Special Agent, beginning a 20-year career. He was an assault team leader and an original member of the FBI's Hostage Rescue Team.

The Navy SEAL Foundation is a highly worthwhile organization. Its health and welfare programs provide tragedy assistance for families when a loved one is killed in combat or training. It also supports SEALs wounded in combat, among other means of support.

With Medal of Honor recipient Master Chief Petty Officer Britt Slabinski.

They collided head-on

In December, 2020, I was dispatched to a traffic collision with major injuries just east of the coastal town of Pescadero.

One of the drivers was still in the car.

I was the first to arrive on scene. The driver of a Porsche, who was following two of his friends, came around a turn covered with black ice, slid into the side of a two-lane bridge, then bounced off into the opposing lane, right into the path of a Dodge Ram pickup truck. They collided head on.

The Porsche driver, seated in a racing-style seat and wearing a four-point harness, was barely conscious, his face covered in blood from his serious facial injuries. I asked him what hurt the most and he said his foot. I looked down at the floorboard and saw his lower left leg had a compound fracture, with bones sticking out. I tried to keep him talking for the next 10 minutes until firefighters arrived.

Removed from the car, placed on a backboard

The firefighters removed the driver from the car and placed him on a backboard. They loaded him into an ambulance and drove him to Pescadero High School, where a landing zone was established. I had grave concerns that he might die as he was being placed in the Life Flight helicopter. Life Flight flew him to Stanford Hospital Trauma Center.

I often wondered how he was doing until a co-worker found a GoFundMe page opened to assist with the driver's recovery.

Although the GoFundMe page had closed, there was the driver's daughter's email address. I emailed her and she put me in touch with the driver's wife. We had a three-way conference call with the driver, Freddie; his wife, Staci; and me.

Freddie told me he suffered from a brain bleed and a broken leg, among other injuries. Doctors placed more than 150 stitches in his face. He spent two and a half weeks at Stanford Hospital and was released early due to the COVID-19 pandemic. He went back to Stanford three months after the crash for another successful surgery on his leg in which surgeons grafted a bone from his femur to his tibia.

- ► Freddie and I are about the same age.
- ► We both drive Porsches.
- ► Freddie and his buddies were driving to a coffee shop in Pescadero, the same coffee shop I responded from.
- ► Freddie and Staci live blocks from Leland High School, in San Jose, where I went to school.

Perhaps it is for these reasons I felt a connection to Freddie and was concerned for him. We continue to stay in touch and recently had lunch together. I feel good about reaching out to Freddie and believe it is the first time doing so in my career.

Cops and firefighters respond to so many calls like this, never knowing how they end. I am so pleased that this call had the best possible outcome and Freddie is recovering.

Extraditions to Ohio and Oklahoma

We would occasionally be offered or assigned an extradition when I was a deputy with the San Mateo County Courts and Transportation Bureau. Extraditions are trips to pick up an inmate who is being held in another jurisdiction on a warrant from our county.

Sometimes they were long day trips or overnight driving trips to neighboring states. And, if the stars are aligned correctly, we would fly someplace fun like New York City or Honolulu, allowing an extra day on our own time to sightsee. Usually the hottest destinations were assigned to senior deputies.

I was assigned a trip to Cleveland, Ohio, in July, 2019. Since the inmate I would pick up was female, my partner for the extradition was Deputy Jennifer Schwartz. Jennifer had been with the division for many years before my arrival at the sheriff's office, so together we navigated the sometimes complicated and convoluted process of flying armed and returning with a prisoner.

Cleveland might not have been a destination to be grabbed up by senior deputies, but Jennifer had been there before and we hit a few attractions on our off day. We started at the Rock & Roll Hall of Fame where we saw Michael Jackson's sequined glove, Janis Joplin's VW Bug and one of Jimi Hendricks' many guitars.

There was a fleet of tall sailing ships in town as part of a larger annual Tall Ships Festival, so we visited a few ships in the sweltering heat. That night we went to a Cleveland Indians game, which ended with a video rock show and amazing fireworks. The stadium seemed pumped up since Cleveland was the host city for the Major League Baseball All Star Weekend starting the next day.

The inmate we picked up the next morning was a young woman from the area who had been visiting the San Francisco Bay Area trying to "come up" as she described it, when she got mixed up in using stolen credit cards, then didn't make it back to San Mateo County for court. That's why the judge issued a warrant.

A police officer discovered that she had a warrant from San Mateo County when he pulled her over for speeding. She had been living with her family near Cleveland. She was a polite young woman, which was a good thing, because when you're picking up an inmate to take across the country on an airplane, you always hope they're the cooperative type.

Not a major tourist attraction

In December, 2019, Deputy Schwartz and I partnered up again for an adventure to the South. Marietta, Oklahoma, was our destination to pick up a female inmate who had a warrant for transporting marijuana. Marietta, with a population of under 3,000, wasn't really a major tourist attraction, so we decided to go to Dallas, only 90 minutes over the border.

Downtown Dallas was bustling with tourists. We mostly walked around, taking in what we could close to our hotel. President John Fitzgerald Kennedy was assassinated in Dallas on Nov. 22, 1963. We stood on the Grassy Knoll and tried to visit the School Book Depository Museum, but we had no reservations, so we only could make it as far as the Museum Store. We took a tour of Reunion Tower instead. It offered some great views of Dealey Plaza and the rest of downtown Dallas. There's something slightly eerie about standing in such a significant place in U.S. history.

It's important to remember that Officer J.D. Tippit of the Dallas Police Dept. also lost his life that same day while questioning assassin Lee Harvey Oswald.

Death by doctors

Medical malpractice is the third leading cause of death in this country, according to the peer-reviewed *Journal of the American Medical Association*. It trails only heart disease and cancer.

Death by doctors.

Doctors are better educated than most police officers, operate in a sterile environment, and usually have the luxury of preparing their medical strategies.

Contrast that with police officers. We are called upon to react and make split-second decisions in often dynamic, dangerous, chaotic, and rapidly evolving situations. Police officers are severely disadvantaged. Could we get it right more often than doctors?

When a doctor or other health care provider deviates from the widely recognized standard of care and harms the patient, that is medical malpractice. The standard of care is what a reasonable health care provider would have done in the same circumstances. If the provider fails, this could be medical negligence.

When cops use any amount of force, it looks bad on TV news

The current environment is not conducive to aggressive law enforcement, not that the crooks aren't still victimizing innocent people, stealing anything that isn't nailed down, and violating conditions of their probation or parole, but when cops use pretty much any type of force it looks bad. It's hard to get around it.

We are well aware that we will never get into trouble for the traffic stop we never make. We wonder why we should put ourselves through the scrutiny and aggravation of engaging a criminal with force when the incident could be the lead story on the nightly television news broadcast.

In July, 2020, Berkeley passed legislation transferring traffic enforcement responsibilities from the cops to unarmed non-law enforcement employees. Other cities around the country are considering the same change.

I certainly hope that this experiment does not result in the death of a civilian.

How will the criminals know if they are being stopped by a real police officer or a civilian? Will criminals even care who is stopping them? Traffic enforcement stops are among the most dangerous of police duties. The unknown factor puts officers in a very precarious situation. Is the driver a wanted fugitive? Did the driver just commit a violent crime? The list of other dangerous possibilities is almost endless.

In the May, 1991 issue of the American Rifleman published an article headlined "Cop Is Not a Dirty Word" by Harlon Carter, former chief of the U.S. Border Patrol.

He states, "This book is a comprehensive study of the problem of police malpractice." He said he has no interest except reporting on police malpractice.

Criminal violence by police officers should not be tolerated. When violence by police officers is identified, they should be charged, given a fair trial, and, if found guilty, given the appropriate sentence."

But there is another side to the issue.

Asking the same question every day

The legendary Los Angeles Chief of Police William H. Parker, undeniably regarded by his own officers as a tough disciplinarian, told the California Peace Officers Assn. in 1956: "A dangerous custom has arisen in America wherein the hapless police officer is a defenseless target of ridicule and abuse from every quarter. It is destroying its ability to protect itself by discouraging those qualified from taking up the police service as a career and creating such an uncertainty in the mind of the police officer as to what is appropriate action to the extent that inaction may become the order of the day."

I find this observation by Chief Parker most insightful. Nearly 65 years later, this dilemma is still relevant.

How many police officers ask these very questions every day? How many qualified candidates reluctantly abandon the idea of becoming a police officer because of a possible onslaught of ridicule and abuse?

Unfortunately, suspects have a lot of input about how a law enforcement contact will play out. Police officers are increasingly finding creative ways to de-escalate potentially violent encounters, but know the suspect may not have any interest in de-escalating.

These are the situations that often appear as the lead story on the nightly news or in social media.

Of course, police officers have the option not to arrest an uncooperative or combative suspect. The response of "we'll get him another day" is gaining traction.

Have we as a society come to the position whereby suspects are empowered to decide if they are going to be arrested or not? And, if this is where we are headed, would it embolden criminals? And, when that another day does come and the suspect still doesn't want to be arrested, do police officers acquiesce and perhaps wait for yet another day? Is this becoming the new normal?

Police officers deserve to know that expectations have been lowered. What are society's new expectations of officers? Who ultimately decides who gets arrested, cops or criminal?

With my two sons. Do you see a public-service pattern here?

My sons, Jeffrey and Gregory, chose public service

My wife, Donna, and I are fortunate to have two wonderful sons, Jeffrey and Gregory. Both have chosen careers in public service. Jeffrey is a captain with the Pasadena Fire Dept. and is trained as a paramedic. Gregory is a motorcycle officer with the Daly City Police Dept.

This is exactly what they wanted to do since they were young boys. Right out of high school, Gregory enlisted in the Marine Corps Reserve and completed his eight-year contract, then enlisted in the Coast Guard Reserve, serving in maritime law enforcement.

When my sons were young they rode in the patrol car with me and other officers like I rode with my father. Obviously, Gregory was bitten by the law enforcement bug. He became a Millbrae police explorer when he was 17.

Donna has strongly supported me being in law enforcement and the military at the same time. Both professions required me being away from home. My overseas deployment required me being way for a year and a half. At the time Jeffrey was 17 and Gregory was 14. Donna did a great job of being both mother and father during my absences.

The police are the public and the public are the police

Sir Robert Peel, the first metropolitan police chief in London, England, is credited with nine insightful principles of effective policing. He is the reason that London police officers are called "Bobbies" or "Peelers." Sir Robert Peel was way ahead of his time.

- ▶ *PRINCIPLE 1: "The basic mission for which the police exist is to prevent crime and disorder."*
- ▶ *PRINCIPLE 2: "The ability of the police to perform their duties is dependent upon public approval of police actions."*

- ► PRINCIPLE 3: *"Police must secure the willing cooperation of the public in voluntary observance of the law to be able to secure and maintain the respect of the public."*
- ► PRINCIPLE 4: *"The degree of cooperation of the public that can be secured diminishes proportionately to the necessity of the use of physical force."*
- ► PRINCIPLE 5: *"Police seek and preserve public favor not by catering to the public opinion but by constantly demonstrating absolute impartial service to the law."*
- ► PRINCIPLE 6: *"Police use physical force to the extent necessary to secure observance of the law or to restore order only when the exercise of persuasion, advice and warning is found to be insufficient."*
- ► PRINCIPLE 7: *"Police, at all times, should maintain a relationship with the public that gives reality to the historic tradition that the police are the public and the public are the police; the police being only members of the public who are paid to give full-time attention to duties which are incumbent on every citizen in the interests of community welfare and existence."*
- ► PRINCIPLE 8: *"Police should always direct their action strictly towards their functions and never appear to usurp the powers of the judiciary."*
- ► PRINCIPLE 9: *"The test of police efficiency is the absence of crime and disorder, not the visible evidence of police action in dealing with it."*

Sir Robert Peel's nine principles of policing are just as relevant today as they were in 1829. Effective policing is really all about relationships with the entire cross section of the community: residents, merchants, school staff, visitors, and service clubs, to name a few.

The statement "The police are the public and the public are the police" rings true. You can't have one without the other.

The Grogan family: Jeffrey in his fire turnouts, my wife, Donna, me, and Gregory in his police uniform.

His perfect combination of charisma and character

While with the Millbrae police, I had the privilege of working with the late Officer John Marty. John was a special man, a one in a million.

People gravitated to his perfect combination of charisma and character. John was a natural at community policing. He helped folks in the community as a police officer with the myriad of situations that officers are called upon to resolve. That is what John enjoyed doing and what he excelled at.

Because of John's outgoing personality and involvement with his children's school and sports events, he had a huge positive impact on the people in Millbrae. When people needed an officer, John was very often the first they called upon.

Early on in my career, I was watching John's style, but was more focused on putting bad guys in jail. However, as I became more seasoned, it became apparent that because of all the relationships John cultivated, his legacy would live on far beyond mine. Sir Robert Peel would have liked John as a member of his department.

Chapter 7

In Conclusion

It is a privilege to wear the badge. It is a symbol of public trust.

The law enforcement profession has been under fire and very much in the public eye during the past several decades or perhaps even longer, and I am more deeply committed to my chosen vocation.

I am fully aware of the weaknesses and human frailty within our ranks. However, I am equally aware of the extraordinary, unwavering bravery, dedication and self-sacrifice my fellow officers show every day.

Some semblance of peace and order

Law enforcement recruits from the human race, so it will always be a challenge to identify the rare bad apples and take care of the situation. Nevertheless, day in and day out, we are struggling to maintain some semblance of peace and order in a very troubled and violent society.

Despite our human frailty, we get it right most of the time. I would encourage everyone to ride with their local law enforcement agency. The opportunity to see, first hand, what is expected from their law enforcement officers and how often they actually deliver will be worthwhile.

Despite choosing to witness the dark side of life, I have maintained a sense of humor, avoiding burnout and becoming cynical. Overall, I believe police work is a young person's job, although maturity and experience have their place.

Still pushing a patrol car

At 59, I am still pushing a patrol car up and down the San Mateo County coast. With the combination of my age and the current political environment where cops are being scrutinized for their split-second decisions, many of which are captured on body camera, being reactive is just fine for now, but I did not become a cop to be reactive.

I still find the job rewarding. I particularly like interacting with the farmers and ranchers out on the coast. Most of the coast is rural and a refreshing change from city policing. In high school I was in the Future Farmers of America. This may account for why interacting with the ranchers and farmers is so enjoyable and refreshing.

Fundamentally, the police are tasked with preventing crime, keeping the peace, and making arrests. For the safety of the public, I believe it is imperative that criminals thoroughly understand that cops are not passively watching them, but are committed to interrupting their behavior when they break the law. It is true we are not going to necessarily arrest our way out of the crime problem. However, putting criminals in jail will always be a slice of the solution.

Here are only a few of the many root causes of crime:

► *Drugs*
► *Family conditions*
► *Hatred*
► *Housing*
► *Lack of education*
► *Mental illness*
► *Peer pressure*
► *Politics*
► *Poverty*
► *Religion*
► *Society*
► *Unemployment*

It is unrealistic to hold law enforcement responsible for the array of factors and individual problems that contribute to crime. Parents, schools, churches, community organizations, individual responsibility, friends, and families have to take ownership in addressing how to be respectful, kind, and productive members of society.

Police body cameras and cell phone cameras are allowing the public to witness what results when people decide to resist arrest. And, yes, some of these recordings show when both criminals and police use excessive force.

Each use-of-force situation is unique.

Police officers are not exempt from the law. When police officers are found to cross the line from reasonable force to excessive force they are disciplined, sometimes losing their jobs, and often prosecuted.

The use of force must constantly be evaluated.

Did the suspect have intent, opportunity, and ability? A professional boxer certainly has the ability to create a lot of harm, but if he is in a cell by himself or 25 yards away does he have the opportunity to hurt anyone? No. Even though he may still have intent and ability, the opportunity leg of the three-legged stool is missing. Without all three legs, the stool does not stand.

Police make most arrests without incident

Each use-of-force situation is unique.

Most arrests, day in and day out, are made without incident. Some arrests involve the use of some minimal force. Some fall into the category of an intermediate force option. These are incidents in the continuum between simple control holds, such as a twist lock or arm bar, and the use of deadly force, such as a firearm.

Examples of intermediate force options are a Taser, pepper spray, a flashlight, or an impact weapon such as a straight or expandable baton. Police use deadly force to save the life of an innocent person, a police officer, or both.

The use of deadly force is by far the exception. The vast majority of officers, like me, have never used deadly force in their entire career, or, in my case, a very long career.

There is a social experiment going on to minimize the consequences of criminal behavior and hold cops more accountable. Yes, the crooks are being held less accountable and the cops more accountable. You read that right. I believe and hope this is temporary.

State prisoners are being released early; many re-offend and return to prison. It would be best if they were released when they are rehabilitated and able to become productive members of society. When prisoners are released from custody, they should be set up for success. Otherwise, they will fall back to the same behavior that put them into prison in the first place.

I remember looking forward to my father coming home from his CHP job and hearing his stories about his day. Cops are trying to survive not only literally but also emotionally. Unfortunately, inaction is the safest way to survive this period of being scrutinized for any use of force. There is a small percentage of criminals who do not want to go back to jail and are willing to do virtually anything not to be arrested.

A smooth-talking, seasoned officer oozing with diplomacy

These criminals are really challenging. Like most seasoned officers, I can normally talk people into handcuffs. Cops become very persuasive and develop keen verbal skills, becoming masters of finesse. They are consummate problem solvers. They have developed the ability to talk with anyone at the person's level. Some people call it the gift of gab, being a smooth talker, or having a silver tongue. The goal is to avoid a physical confrontation.

But there is no guarantee a parolee who does not want to return to prison will listen to reason from anyone, including a smooth-talking, seasoned officer oozing with diplomacy.

Law enforcement requires split-second decision making. A suspect's action will always beat an officer's reaction, putting cops in a vulnerable, disadvantaged position. Cops are often trying to play catch-up when confronted with a violent attack.

Hard to get, easy to lose

I view the job as a vocation rather than just an occupation. The job is one of the hardest to get but the easiest to lose.

What other profession requires successful completion of a written test, oral interview, psychological test, background investigation, polygraph examination, medical screening, physical agility test, completion of a six-month academy, and a three-month field training program followed by a probationary period of a year or longer?

Cops are accountable for their actions both on duty and off duty, every day, around the clock.

Nearly every cop I've met joined the profession for the right reason; they wanted to help people. Like any other profession, some bad apples make it through the protracted testing process and become cops. These are the ones who tarnish the badge and end up disciplined.

Body cameras have been a game changer. I didn't like the new technology at first, but now I would not work without one. The things we often see are hard to believe. Having a recording verifies what sometimes is almost unbelievable. Often the people we interact with are emotionally at their very worst. They may be drunk, on drugs, or a combination of both. They are often embarrassed when they see themselves on the body camera video.

Adrenaline management

As a young officer, I had no idea how adrenaline, a very powerful stress hormone, affects the body. I was 10 years into my career when the concept of adrenaline management became popular. I would encourage new officers to become aware how adrenaline can take over and cause an officer to act in ways she or he normally wouldn't or even shouldn't.

Understanding and recognizing when fellow officers are caught up with adrenaline rushes can save an officer's career. Officers are duty-bound to stop a fellow officer when she or he has crossed the line from using reasonable force to excessive force.

I know I have gotten caught up in the moment and did things I should not have because of adrenaline. Having a thorough understanding of what adrenaline is capable of doing to our judgment can significantly improve use-of-force encounters.

Some of the most profound adrenaline rushes were at the end of vehicle pursuits. The combination of the siren, high speeds, and demanding driving conditions have a unique way of getting the adrenaline going like nothing I have ever experienced. Criminals, too, are affected by adrenaline, as well as mental illness, or whatever they may have ingested or injected. Sometimes the combination of adrenaline, drugs and mental illness are involved.

In so many ways, I thoroughly enjoyed the job. I was so fortunate to have not just an occupation but a vocation for 40 years. The job really is like having ringside tickets to the greatest show on earth. Just when I thought I pretty much saw it all, some new twist would pop up.

Learning how criminals think

I was able to hone my keen sense of who is likely a criminal and who is not. I was free to follow my instincts, interact with a lot of criminals, learn how they think, befriend them, and learn what tactics they use to avoid being arrested. All this resulted in a solid amount self-initiated activity. When I think back on all the crazy situations I was involved in, I realize that I am lucky to be able tell my story.

I believe really effective cops develop a sixth sense for spotting criminals. They pick up on subtle mannerisms such as:

- ► *Avoiding looking at cop or a patrol car.*
- ► *Lighting a cigarette when being pulled over.*
- ► *Avoiding pulling out in front of a patrol car at an intersection.*
- ► *Making an unusual sudden turn when being followed by a patrol car.*
- ► *Stopping when being followed by a patrol car before the officer uses the siren.*

It works the other way. The outlaw motorcycle gang members proudly display their patches on the back of their jackets or vests. Seasoned criminals also develop a sixth sense and can spot a cop who is out of uniform and off-duty. Criminals have told me cops just carry themselves a certain confident way.

I know my service to community and country is coming to an end, at least in my current job.

Trying to fill the void

It is becoming very clear to me that I am emotionally over-invested in police work. The job seduced me away from my personal life. It became who I am. It still is. I am desperately trying to find something to fill the void I will create by leaving the best vocation in the world.

The combination of being a cop and military service member made for an exciting and rewarding journey of 40 plus years. I have been so lucky to experience the strong camaraderie unique to law enforcement and the military.

In the final analysis, it is the wonderful relationships we experience along the way that really matter. Crossing the finish line safely, healthy, and emotionally intact will be a great personal and professional accomplishment. I will take it one day at a time and be open to whatever comes my way.

About the Author

Michael Grogan is a third-generation law enforcement officer on duty in the San Francisco Bay Area for over 40 years. He worked for two city police departments and is now a deputy sheriff with the San Mateo County Sheriff's Office.

He spent 22 years in the military as a special agent with the Coast Guard Investigative Service and the Army Criminal Investigation Division, investigating felony-level crimes in Iraq and Afghanistan.

He was also assigned to the Pentagon, where he provided worldwide protection to the top Dept. of Defense officials. He is a graduate of the FBI National Academy, 200th Session, Quantico, Virginia.

Shortly after the September 11, 2001, terrorist attacks on our country, Reserve Coast Guard Investigative Service Special Agent Michael Grogan received active duty orders and became one of the Coast Guard's first sea marshals. Sea marshals were tasked with preventing terrorists from taking control of ships and running them into the Golden Gate Bridge, other vessels, a pier, or other target of opportunity.

Grogan and his fellow sea marshals realized that even crew members could be supporters of Al Qaeda or affiliated with that terrorist organization. The ships that sea marshals protected consisted of oil tankers, container ships, cruise ships, and bulk carriers from around the world.

Grogan transferred military branches and became an Army Criminal Investigation Division special agent serving in several active duty assignments that included Iraq, Afghanistan, and the Pentagon. After 22 years of military service, he retired at the rank of Chief Warrant Officer 3.

When he was 19, he worked as a reserve police officer for the Los Gatos Police Dept. At 20, he began a 30-year career with the Millbrae Police Dept. and retired at the rank of captain.

He faced two of the greatest tragedies of his life while with the department, the on-duty murder of a close friend and fellow police officer and the drowning of a baby boy whom he drove lights and sirens to the hospital, but could not save.

# # #

Acknowledgements

In March 2021, I heard Anne Lamott of Marin County, California, a highly accomplished writer, public speaker, and teacher, speaking on a National Public Radio program. She was encouraging listeners to write books.

She said a writer needs to commit to writing an hour or two every day and don't wait to be in the mood to write as she has never been in the mood to write. She provided other tips for aspiring authors, but only these two pointers stuck with me. After taking her advice to heart, I realized I could be disciplined enough to see this project through to completion.

For many years, I wanted to capture my life's journey in a book for my two sons to read and share with their children someday. What I didn't know then was that it would be one of the most heart-wrenching and painful journeys in my entire life.

Looking back on one's entire life is seldom easy. Our instinct allows us to ignore the bad and retain the good. Writing a memoir often requires one to reflect on both.

After a great deal of self-examination, I purposely left out some experiences as I am still trying to come to terms with them.

I would imagine even the best authors sometimes need a little help in telling their stories. I, on the other hand, required a lot of guidance and received such support from Jan Ford of Jan Ford Public Relations in Palo Alto, California. Her thoughtful expertise and patience were invaluable. I consider Jan one of my dearest friends. She clearly demonstrated her editing and publishing genius with helping me tell my story.

This book is dedicated to all the first responders and military service members who stand watch every hour of every day of every year. Their unwavering dedication to public service is often taken for granted.

I could never have gotten through the process without the love, encouragement, and support of my wife, Donna. Every bit of my spare time went into this memoir and took time away from being with her.

CPSIA information can be obtained
at www.ICGtesting.com
Printed in the USA
LVHW071508070322
712799LV00010B/168

9 781662 460043